Queen Mary's Stair & other stories

ALEX MARKS

Copyright © 2016 Alex Marks
All rights reserved.
ISBN: 1537469797
ISBN-13: 978-1537469799

To Mum, who never understood why I liked to think about frightening things, but who was always at my side if I did.

CONTENTS

Author's note	i
Queen Mary's Stair	1
The Buckled Shoe	50
Sweetie	74
Mine	93
The Undertakers	106
Sign Here	115
Dr Paignton	129

AUTHOR'S NOTE

I have always been fascinated by what's not seen, what lies around the corner, or up the stairs, or right behind you. As a kid, I loved to look at all the garish covers of the horror paperbacks in Woolworths and give myself a fright, and I adored those 1970s TV shows where ghosts ruled, or people from other dimensions had adventures.

Now that I am all grown up (and old enough to know better) I wanted to share some of my macabre imaginings with everyone else. To that end, I've gathered together a few of my favourite creepy stories to make sure you sleep as badly at night as I do.

I hope you like them.

Follow me on Twitter @IamAlexMarks and on my blog iamalexmarks.tumblr.com

QUEEN MARY'S STAIR

Jack Benson had dealt with many stroppy customers in his time. Selling high-end reclaimed building materials inevitably meant he was always brushing up against wealthy, well-educated stockbrokers, bankers, interior decorators and other confident, opinionated souls. He was the nearest thing to an expert many of them would meet in their lives, but nevertheless they still seemed to see it as an irrevocable rule of free-market economics that they should screw every penny from his humble business.

'What's your best price on this?' they'd ask, having seen people saying that on the telly and liking how the question made them look. Jack was fortunately unflappable; just smiling politely as he rolled his cigarette and waited till

Amanda or Guy or Bruno had got bored with posturing and were ready to seal the deal. And besides, he knew he'd bought the roof tiles or balustrades or mirrors for a song and had already added a hefty whack to the price, so he could suck his teeth and 'reluctantly' pantomime a reduction while still making an obscene profit. And Amanda or Guy or Bruno would be able to boast about their own cleverness and tell their friends that they too should go to Benson's when they were renovating their Cotswolds or Thames-side or Devon mansion, and so the great cycle of commerce would turn ever onwards.

But this morning, as he was rolling his fag, Jack was thinking that this particular customer was actually becoming quite annoying. For a change, he wasn't a banker (except in the most colloquial sense) but was some kind of rich geek from a tech company Jack had never heard of. Introduced only as Dave, he was displaying all the other elements of knobbery, happily wasting half an hour pontificating about the difference between a pilaster and a canton. He stood with his hands on his hips, showing off his gym-buffed chest under an original Grateful Dead Europe 72 tour t-shirt, attempting to top this display of confident ignorance by insisting that the parquet floor that Jack knew for a certain fact had been lifted from an Edwardian school in Hertfordshire was nothing more than a cheap fake.

'Cheeky fucker,' thought Jack in the private sanctum of his mind, whilst his fingers rolled his ciggie tighter and tighter as if it were his customer's neck.

'So what else do you have for me?' Dave swaggered off into the dingy recesses of the warehouse, highly pleased with his display of superiority. He ignored Jack's invitation to enter a room filled with doors of all shapes and sizes, and instead began to clamber roughly over stacks of dusty chairs to get into a particularly inaccessible corner. 'What's over here?' His tone, whether intentionally or otherwise, rang with the accusation that something marvellous must be being kept from him. He struggled on and ripped down a yellowing tarp, revealing a series of solid wooden pieces that didn't look much like anything.

'Staircase,' replied Jack shortly. 'Did you mention you were on the look out for some stairs?'

Dave grinned widely and patronisingly. 'I'll worry about whether I'm interested or not, you just show me what you've got, alright?'

'Arsehole,' thought Jack.

'Arsehole,' thought Dave.

The two men stood and looked at the collection of heavy oak sections in silence. Dust choked deep mouldings and a scattering of tiny holes showed that woodworm had lived there at some point, but for all that anyone could see this had once been a thing of great expense and quality.

'It's a complete staircase with balustrade and side panels, two flights clockwise,' said Jack.

'What wood is this?' asked Dave, running his finger over the grain. 'Elm?'

'Oak.' Jack suppressed a smile at this tiny point scored, and reminded himself that the real victory would be in separating this annoying ponce from several thousands of pounds. He went on in a more helpful tone. 'It comes with all the spindles, newels and handrails.'

Dave was standing back with an unimpressed air but Jack could tell he was hooked. 'How old is it, and where did it come from?'

'It's old, dates to about 1550. And it came from Warrington Hall just up the road.'

'Wait a minute, wait a minute...' Dave's smile was shark-like. 'Warrington Hall was that Victorian gothic monstrosity that burned down, wasn't it?' He nodded to himself gleefully. 'So don't try to fucking kid me that this is Tudor, ok?'

Jack looked on impassively. He found this man and his enormous ego highly distasteful, and this was probably the reason that he decided, on the spot, to sell him the staircase. Given its history he'd been reluctant to pass it on, but now - well.

'You're absolutely right that Warrington Hall was constructed in the 1880s in the Gothic Revival style,' he said, his annoyance letting his expertise show for once, 'but it incorporated many structural and decorative elements bought from earlier buildings. This staircase was one such. Originally it was installed in Douglas Castle in the Borders.'

Dave listened. He seemed to rather reluctantly change his mind; perhaps this idiot wasn't out to cheat him after all. Amongst this inner monologue, a bell of memory faintly rang.

'Douglas Castle? Wasn't that where Mary, Queen of Scots was imprisoned?'

'One of the places.' Jack cast his client a sideways look and took the plunge. 'The story goes that when the staircase was assembled at Warrington, her ghost could be seen, walking up and down. Queen Mary's stair, it was called.'

'Huh!' What superstitious morons people were, thought Dave. He liked the idea of owning a staircase that more ignorant souls had whispered about. He would laugh at that every day.

'What a supercilious moron he is,' thought Jack. He could see the other man was quite taken with proving his superiority in solid oak.

He could tell him the rest of it, but hey, he was busy.

'Ok,' said Dave, 'what's your best price?'

The staircase, it seemed, didn't want to be moved. Or maybe, thought Jack as he sucked a bruised thumb and glared at the large, difficult pieces, it was just trying to be as bloody awkward as possible. Any doubts he might have had about the ethics of selling the thing dissolved rapidly: he wanted rid. He and his young assistants hefted and wrenched and pulled and shoved it away from its position and slowly across the warehouse floor, before loading it into the lorry that Dave had sent to collect his prize. As the back panels were laced tightly shut and the vehicle inched its way out of Benson's Reclamation, the proprietor released a breath he hadn't realised he'd been holding.

'Thank God for that,' he said.

The truck got as far as the nearest motorway interchange and broke down. The engine refused to restart, and in the end the cab was towed off and another backed into the traces in its stead, and the staircase resumed its journey to its new home. Five miles out and with darkness falling the back axel snapped, marooning the HGV at the side of a country lane, canted at a perilous angle. In the morning, yet another lorry was dispatched to take over, and again the heavy oak sections were unloaded and reloaded, doors were slammed and finally the Queen Mary's stair made its entrance at the neat Georgian manor that Dave was busy renovating.

The master of the house was away on some important business overseas, so it was his wife, Billie, who took delivery of the stairs and oversaw the slow job of unloading its pieces from the van and carrying them into the wide entrance hall. The house had been turned into a school during the 1960s, with many of its original features ripped out and substituted for deliberately ugly utilitarian versions, but now this new staircase would replace the open-backed monstrosity that marred this generous space. And, according to the superstitions that her husband had gleefully told her about, it would be a talking point in its own right as well. Dave had shown her all the photos, and had dug out of the digital archives images from its most recent resting place at Warrington Hall. Billie had thought it rather dark and sombre, but she knew better than to try to persuade her husband to change his mind; besides, he'd already paid for the thing. And as usual he'd swanned off on one of his many trips, leaving her to do the hard work of getting it all installed and ready for his impatient inspection when he returned. He'd already texted her three times that morning, wanting to know whether it had finally made it to their house. She was relieved to be able to send a quick message announcing simply: 'It's here'.

During the next few weeks the carpenters laboured to restore the mistreated segments of old oak. The brown-carpeted steps were ripped out, and in their place the Tudor stairs rose steadily, every day bringing a new section into use. The balusters were slotted in, the handrail polished, the steps and risers (Billie now knew all the lingo) adjusted until they were perfectly aligned. The last stage was dropping the huge, heavily-carved newel post into its waiting space; Josef and his band of chippies were pleased to have got to the end of this job and were laughing as they manhandled the two hundred kilo beam of black wood upright and inched it towards its resting place. Billie stood nearby, recording the process on her iPhone.

'Got the weight?' Joe called up to his ginger-haired apprentice, Peter, who was holding the end of a strong tape, wrapped around the heavy oak, and keeping it upright.

'It's all good,' called Pete, laughing and taking another twist of the webbing around his wrist.

'Keep well back,' warned his boss, and the young man squared his feet and braced against the heavy handrail.

At ground level, the men walked the post forward a bit, and then it jammed.

'Bit of lift,'

'Right,'

'Steady, push that side...'

The camera recorded shufflings and gruntings, a grimace on the face of one of the workmen as he shoved at the stuck bit of wood. Deep carvings of birds and flowers glinted in the soft afternoon light.

'Bit more... bit more...'

Quicker than anyone expected the enormous block tipped into the slot in the stairs and dropped. The tape, which half a second before had been holding it loosely upright, now snapped taut with the sound of a whiplash and pulled down on the arm of the lad standing above on the landing. On the video, seen afterwards by the coroner, there was a moment were shocked faces were seen, a snapshot, then Peter just appeared as if from nowhere, arrowing down, head-first, onto the black and white marble floor. Death by misadventure, said the coroner; 'Teenager dies in freak accident', said the local paper; Josef said nothing, just packing up his gear and his team and leaving silently, with only a dark glance cast at the completed staircase.

'Fucking amateurs!' ranted Dave, back from his trip and incandescent that he'd been forced to attend the coroner's hearing. He had got rich so he wouldn't be forced to do anything, and now, today, he'd had to put on a suit and sit and be lectured by some washed out nobody who probably didn't earn in a whole year what Dave brought in during a slow afternoon. 'You should have employed somebody who knew what they were doing!'

Billie was looking pale. She had seen Peter fall, and kept seeing it, in fact, every time she closed her eyes. 'It wasn't Josef's fault, it was an accident.' She shook her head and took a long drink from her gin and tonic. 'Nobody could understand it, how he came to slip and get over the bannister…'

Dave wasn't listening. 'And now this house has been in all the papers, and everyone's talking about the curse of Mary Queen of Scots! Where the hell did they get that from, eh?' He flung a newspaper down, angrily.

'I don't know! You were telling everyone about it when you bought the bloody staircase so it got about. Everyone knows.'

Dave's face went white with rage. 'Don't you blame me for this, you cow!' He jabbed a finger at his wife and, despite herself, she flinched. 'Just finish the damn renovations and don't mess it up again!' He grabbed his jacket and his retro courier bag. 'I'm going to the office. I'll be back at the weekend.'

Billie was quite relieved that Dave had gone. The other workmen had taken the day off as a mark of respect to poor Peter, and for once she was alone. She let out a huge breath. The silence was soothing.

Out of habit she made herself a simple dinner and then cleared up. Walking round the house to make sure all the doors and windows were locked took ages, but it was her job and she was used to it. The painters were almost the only tradesmen left now, and even they were coming to the end of their work; it was going to be strange to consider that the house was actually finished. What was she going to do with her time then?

Billie checked the front door and then walked slowly up the stairs. She was looking at the big, modern chandelier that Dave had commissioned (at huge expense) for the ceiling in the entrance hall. It was a fat cluster of oversize lightbulbs, each with a curly, glowing filament inside, and each costing a staggering amount of money. Fortunately it had been installed without any breakages, or any accidents, and she had to admit that it was an attractive feature – drawing the eye as she climbed up and around the dark stairs. She got to the top and stopped where the handrail showed tiny signs of having been repaired: this was where Peter had fallen. Even now she couldn't believe it had actually happened, that the weight of the newel post had somehow jerked him over the bannister. Standing here she was almost at a level with the chandelier and so she heard it distinctly when one of the big bulbs went suddenly dark with a subtle pop. Bugger it, thought Billie, and she stared at the darkened glass as if willing it to come on again and save her explaining to Dave that it had blown. Then a movement caught the corner of her eye and her head turned automatically towards it.

A woman was walking up the stairs. She was quite short and was wearing a dark blue dress of some stiff fabric and with a flash of something white at the throat. Another piece of white cloth covered her head, giving it a strangely square outline. Billie stared. She saw the woman's face clearly: pale, worried, but very beautiful. The woman didn't seem to have noticed her, and as Billie heard her pulse start to pound in her ears the figure turned the corner on the stair and went to step up onto the landing beside her.

And then she simply wasn't there.

Billie took three steps back and stood, trembling, with her hand across her mouth. She was suddenly very aware of all of the house's empty rooms, all the closed doors and cupboards and darkened spaces, all the corners and attics and hallways. She resisted for a second, and then turned and bolted along the landing and into her own suite of rooms, slamming and locking the door and turning on the telly and all the lights and dialling her husband's number with shaking fingers. Luckily it went to voicemail, and at the sound of Dave's impatient message Billie snapped back to herself and hung up, overwhelmingly grateful that he hadn't answered and allowed her to blurt out what had just happened. She sat on the edge of the bed and tried to calm down. It was just her imagination, and after all the stress of the last week who could blame her for seeing things. She just needed a good night's sleep and in the morning she'd laugh about this. She checked the door twice, took an anti-histamine tablet, and then fell asleep with the lights and the TV on.

Out on the landing, the figure in the dark blue dress began to walk back down the stair.

Billie did not see the woman again the next day, nor the day after. She did walk up and down the stairs quite quickly, it's true, but that was just because she was busy getting the house finished and ready for the party that Dave had suddenly decided they should throw for their friends and neighbours. He had gone to New York, so she knuckled down and got the painters finished and the gardeners in, and arranged with some caterers and a band and sent out the invitations. With all of that going on it was perfectly understandable that she didn't look left or right when she was climbing or descending the staircase, and didn't linger on the landing after dark. She knew that sometimes she'd felt a trembling of a presence on the stairs, a whisper of someone breathing, perhaps, but she had ignored it. It was far better not to think about it.

Dave arrived home, annoyed and jet lagged, three days before the party. He stood grumpily in the entrance hall and surveyed the expensive chandelier, of which another two bulbs had gone dark.

'You should have got the fitters back!' he said crossly to his wife.

'I did, and they recommended getting the voltages checked, and that's been done too.'

'Huh,' Dave couldn't think of anything else that Billie should *obviously* have done and that made him even more irritated. 'Well, it looks crap. We can't have people round with it like this, we'll have to cancel the party.'

Billie was horrified. After all the work she'd put into the arrangements! She knew that that argument would cut no ice with Dave, however, so instead went mercilessly for a weak spot. 'Well, if you think that's best. But you do realise that everyone will assume that it's because of the accident.'

He scowled at her. 'What accident?'

Could he really have forgotten? Or was it that it was just not important enough to be remembered? 'Peter, the apprentice who fell from the landing?' Billie saw a flash of memory chase the temper on her husband's face. 'If we cancel the party now then tongues will wag. They'll say that we're too ashamed to open the house after everything that's happened.'

She had launched her barb, now she stood back and waited for it to hit its mark. Dave fumed for a few more moments and then waved a hand dismissively. 'If you insist on having this party, Billie, then it's up to you. But I can't guarantee to be here.' That was crap, she thought to herself, knowing he would be front and centre with a bottle of champagne and some fake bonhomie, preening himself in his multi-million pound ego project. 'And anyway –'

Dave's words faltered in his throat as they both clearly saw a woman in a dark blue dress step up onto the bottom of the staircase and begin to slowly climb. She held her stiff skirt up from the steps with both hands, and her head was covered by a square white coif that concealed her hair save for a couple of dark red wisps curling by her collar. Billie caught her breath in with a sharp gasp; here she was again! Above their heads, one of the bulbs popped and went dark.

Husband and wife stood in shocked silence and watched the woman turn the corner and start up the final flight to the landing. Then Dave made Billie jump out of her skin by suddenly calling out: 'Hey!'

The shout was loud in the quiet hall and for a second the figure didn't seem to have heard it, but then they saw her cock her head slightly as if listening to something from far away. And her head turned further to look down towards them but her foot hit the top step and she was not there anymore.

There was a heavy silence. Then Dave wheeled round and grabbed Billie by the shoulders. 'Did you see that!' he demanded, 'did you see it?' She nodded, and he whirled away and ran to the bottom of the stairs, peering up. 'Shit! Mary fucking Queen of Scots!'

Billie's heart was still racing. Something about that woman, that figure, absolutely encased her in dread, in a feeling of utter despair, and here was Dave capering about with a huge grin on his face as if he'd managed to win the lottery without ever buying a ticket. She shook herself. If Dave had seen it, then she wasn't going mad after all...

'Have you seen this before?' he was hopping with excitement. She nodded bleakly.

'Unfuckingbelievable!' Dave looked at his vintage Timex watch. 'Eleven o'clock. Eleven o'clock. Was it this time when you saw it?'

Billie cast her mind back and worked it out. 'Probably –' she began. But her husband didn't wait to hear the rest of what she had to say.

'Fuck! Just you wait till everyone sees this at the party!' he crowed. 'My God! Rathie is going to be sick with envy! All that money spent on that dreary castle and not a spook to be seen, and here we are with one that we've imported! Fucking imported!' He howled with laughter, and Billie thought it was a very unpleasant sound. Above their heads, the expensive chandelier buzzed angrily.

The party was a tremendous success. Or so Billie judged, working by her usual yardstick of how Dave was feeling. He had been in a state of enormous excitement all day, fussing over the caterers and getting in the way of the band, and in the end she'd had to practically banish him to his office to do some research on hauntings before he'd pissed everyone off to the point of leaving. Now, resplendent in a bright red Bowie Star Man t-shirt amongst the guests in their black dinner jackets and posh frocks, he stood at the foot of the stairs and held forth. As she drifted to and fro, making sure glasses were filled and egos soothed, important people greeted and their remaining friends actually spoken to, Billie heard soundbites of her husband's boasting:

'…ghost of Mary, Queen of Scots…'

'…imported from Warrington Hall with the stairs…'

'…eleven o'clock…'

James Rathie, business partner, frenemy and perpetual source of the Sirocco of jealousy that roared through Dave's psyche, glided up to her and pecked her on the cheek. Billie noted that he was looking impeccable in his expensive tuxedo, an impeccable and expensive young man adhered to his side.

'Billie, Billie, my darling,' he crooned in his dry Edinburgh voice, 'what's all this nonsense about the ghost of Mary, Queen of Scots? I haven't been able to get a sensible word out of Dave all night.'

Billie took a drink of her champagne and decided that perhaps getting helplessly drunk was the best plan for surviving this evening. She handed the empty glass off to a passing waiter and hooked another. 'It's all true, James,' she said, swallowing a mouthful, and wondering idly why gay men were often so gorgeous. 'We bought this staircase and the ghost has come with it.'

Rathie's perfectly-groomed companion widened his dark gazelle's eyes. 'Really? A proper ghost?'

'But surely –' put in James, ever the realist. Billie held up a hand to forestall his comments.

'I know, I know. Who would believe it? But Dave and I have both seen her, walking up the stairs at eleven p.m. He's been lying in wait for her for the past three nights, trying to get her to speak to him.'

Rathie shook his head in wonderment, perhaps at his partner's unlikely enthusiasm. 'And has she?'

Billie drank deep again, and found her glass empty. She signalled for another. 'Not so far,' she said.

'Oh, look!' said Rathie's date, pointing over their heads, and they turned to see Dave standing half way up the stairs waving his hands and shouting for everyone's attention. Billie pushed through the clustering guests to the front row, aware that James and his boyfriend were right behind.

'Ladies and gentlemen!' Dave's face was flushed with excitement. 'Gather round now, gather round! It's five to eleven and our royal visitor will be joining us shortly!' A ripple of happy laughter cascaded through the group. Billie shivered. 'You've all heard the story of how Mary, Queen of Scots, unhappy wife of Darnley and Bothwell, prisoner of her cousin, Elizabeth the first of England, has come to this house in spectral form, attached in some fashion to this staircase. For the past few nights I've watched her appear at eleven o'clock and walk up these steps before vanishing again…'

'Isn't midnight supposed to be the witching hour?' called a woman. People tittered.

'Maybe she's on Daylight Savings,' drawled an American voice and the laughter became bolder, more mocking. Billie saw Dave's face flush with temper.

'Please, please!' he waved for silence again and twisted to look at the hall clock. It was nearly time. 'You'll see for yourselves in a moment. Feel free to try and record this phenomena on your phones – I've had state of the art video equipment running for the past two nights and haven't been able to capture a clear view of her visit on film, but..' The clock (installed this morning, presumably to add a little extra drama to this evening's performance, thought Billie) began to strike eleven. Dave skipped down the steps and crushed back into the front row, snatching his wife's champagne glass and draining it in one movement. Everyone jostled and held their breath. The clock's golden chime rang out again, and again, counting down. Dave swallowed nervously, and Billie surprised them both by reaching out and taking his hand. Rathie's good-looking and sceptical face was twisted into a disbelieving sneer and he stooped to say –

And then there she was.

The whole room seemed to draw in a gasp of shock. Hands shot into the air holding phones and white spikes of flash jagged across the scene, but the woman in the blue dress walked calmly and unseeingly up the stairs, holding her wide skirts up, and nodding her linen-covered head to herself as she went. Dave bounced on the balls of his feet in pure joy at being proved right. James took half a step forward as if literally not believing his own eyes. Billie just felt sick, the expensive champagne turning to vinegar in her stomach.

The woman turned the corner and began ascending the final flight.

Dave suddenly lurched forward and yelled: 'Stop! Stop!'

The balloon of excitement contained in the crowded guests burst, and a clamour of voices called out 'Hey, your majesty!' or 'Oi!' or 'Mary! Mary!' and even more inane things, a shout of laughter accompanying each new witticism. Billie herself spoke, whispering 'No! Don't!' but no-one heard her.

The woman in the blue dress carried on up the steps and for a moment it seemed that she, again, would hear nothing, see nothing, merely trundle on her well-worn track like the decorative figure on a town hall clock. But then she slowed, hands lowering her skirts, and she turned her head and she looked at them all gathered below her. A total silence fell. Her face, pale, beautiful and something else, something that stilled all their voices and stifled their laughter, surveyed the crowd, looking from one to the next, a slight frown deepening on her brow. For a second it seemed that she might speak, her lips appeared to flex, but as if automatically her foot lifted itself and its dainty slipper pressed down onto the top step and she was gone.

A moment of pure silence filled the hall, and then it erupted in a cheer so loud that the expensive chandelier trembled and two of its bulbs went out, casting a deep shadow across the top of the landing. But no-one cared: Dave was instantly surrounded by people slapping him on the back and shaking his hand as if he had single-handedly called back this spectre from the Great Beyond, and then he was hoisted up onto their shoulders and carried, laughing and waving, away into the dining room. The crowd followed him like a tide, ebbing out of the ornate double doors until only Billie was left. She stood there for a long while, looking up at the pool of darkness at the top of the stairs, and feeling like someone was looking back.

In the morning, Dave stirred and found a terrific hangover occupying the place in his skull where his brain would normally be, and so he decided that he was not getting out of bed today. He had been up till dawn, monitoring the social media outpourings of their guests and crowing with delirious joy when all the retweets of their blurry photos had started

#maryqscots trending. Billie, also very fragile in the robust sunshine of a September morning but who had scraped a few more hours of sleep, managed to drag herself out of bed and into her dressing gown, tottering down to the kitchen to put on a pot of very strong coffee. She had a cup herself, leaning back onto the table and soaking up the yellow light pouring through the bifold doors from the kitchen garden. It was half past ten, and she knew that the cleaners and the caterers would be back at twelve to start clearing up the mess from the night before, so that gave her a perfect half an hour to herself before she'd have to start the business of getting up and dressed and ready to be lady of the house. She slid open the doors and stepped outside.

The garden was warm and sheltered, but there was just the faintest pinch in the air, letting her know that these were the favoured last days of the summer and that autumn was waiting in the wings for its cue. Billie had been particular in choosing her gardening staff and they had done an excellent job, transforming the overgrown walled kitchen garden into a cleared and orderly space. Some of the leaves were just curling and yellow, and some of the beds now empty and showing signs of being prepared for their winter rest. A saucy blackbird posed on the top of the red brick wall and sang his heart out and Billie stopped for a minute to listen, thinking that this was the nearest to happy that she'd been in a very long time. She hadn't been keen on buying this house, but she had to admit she did like it here. And Dave wasn't going to be home all that often. Maybe it was all going to work out.

She went to take another drink of coffee and found her cup was empty; well, she really ought to be getting back and having a shower, so she turned and contentedly walked back down the path towards the kitchen door. As she did so she glanced at the house, and caught a movement in the landing window that took her a moment to parse – and then she stopped dead, and dropped her mug onto the ground. A face was looking down at her, reflected in the glass. It was pale, and beautiful, a woman's face, framed in a square white head covering. It was her.

Billie felt her knees literally trembling and her hands jumped to her mouth as if to hold back a cry. She couldn't look away, her eyes were locked on the eyes of the woman staring scornfully down, the eyes of a queen, displeased at the sudden appearance of the very meanest of her subjects. Billie took an involuntary step back, and the figure seemed to vanish – a hesitant step forward and there she was again, imperious, angry.

'She's in the reflection,' whispered Billie to herself.

The rest of the morning was a blur. Somehow Billie managed to act normally enough to fool the cleaners and the others. She wanted to say something, but found that she just couldn't form the words, and so she spent the whole day hoping that someone would look at her and realise something was wrong, and then perhaps ask her what was the matter. But no-one did.

Dave had been roused from his hangover by a phone call from the National Psychical Society asking to come and study the Mary, Queen of Scots phenomenon. He'd been terrifically happy to deny them any access, calling them idiots and amateurs and charlatans, and then lecturing his wife for forty minutes on how much better he was going to be at investigating. And then the journalists had begun phoning, and suddenly here he was being interviewed for a puff piece on the ten o'clock news! The entrance hall was filled with cables and cameras and people trying to get past, and Billie was seized with a terror that another accident would happen and so re-routed all the tradespeople out of an inconvenient side door instead. They grumbled, but she felt a bit calmer. Perhaps she had imagined seeing the queen this morning, she'd been hungover and tired, after all. Billie clutched this thought to herself and found it comforting. She had almost come to believe it, but then just as the journalists were leaving the front doors slammed seemingly of their own accord and refused to open. This type of domestic annoyance would usually have her husband howling with rage, but today Dave happily phoned the locksmith (on camera) and then wasn't even angry when the man arrived and found the doors opened easily.

'Perhaps we've annoyed Her Majesty with our filming today!' burbled the presenter cheerfully, and everyone laughed.

Finally, when all these people had left and the house was quiet again, Billie managed to grab Dave and explain that she'd seen the ghost this morning, occupying a reflection in the window.

'Not possible,' he said.

'But I saw it!'

He smiled his horrible smile and shook his head. 'Stop going on, Billie, you're being hysterical and imagining things. Just – ' he waved his hand impatiently, at a loss to think of some activity that she might normally do, 'go and pick some fucking flowers or something.' And he closed the door of his office and left her alone in the corridor.

'Screw you, then,' she said, and walked as slowly as she could manage to her own bedroom, without once looking back over her shoulder. As she locked the door, she could swear she could hear, from further inside the house, a mocking laugh.

Over the next couple of weeks Billie's life became unbearable. Every mirror, every glass, every shiny, reflective surface was a torment, and she tried to slink past them, eyes averted, desperate not to see what she knew was lurking inside. A sudden turn or a thoughtless look would reveal *her*, smirking in the reflection, mocking Billie and her helplessness to get away. 'Who's the prisoner now,' thought Dave's wife as she tried for the umpteenth time to get him to listen to her.

It didn't help that her husband was shutting himself more and more in his study, researching and arguing with more experienced researchers, being interviewed for TV and radio, even writing some columns for the broadsheets about his experience as the 'owner' of a celebrity ghost. Aside from her natural dislike for all this self aggrandisement, Billie saw how every boast seemed to transform the face that followed her from mirror to mirror, that looked at her scornfully in the bathroom in the morning, sneered from the still surface of water in the butt in the kitchen garden, and laughed at her reflected in the darkening window pane when she was cooking dinner. That face, which was still the beautiful Queen's face, was something else now – a darker something, a misshapen something, that itself looked out from behind the wide blue eyes like a creature trapped and working out how to get loose.

Billie stood and looked at the staircase, perpetually gloomy under the darkened chandelier whose entire clutch of bulbs were now blown. It was like a diseased organ, she thought to herself, transplanted here and disgorging its infection into the house. And now Mary, of what was left of Mary, or what thought it was Mary, was metastasising and would soon be everywhere. What would she do when she was free?

Dave really enjoyed himself over the next couple of weeks. Truth be told, business had become quite dull, with all sorts of meetings scheduled and papers to read, and he couldn't be arsed with any of that. He'd told James to hold the fort, and had happily spent thousands on high-tech surveillance equipment, thermal cameras, and tiny piezo vibration detectors which he'd placed under the stair carpet at several points. The ghost had continued to appear at eleven every night, but he hadn't managed to get her to speak and the readings from all his gizmos were ambiguous. It was frustrating, but he knew he would be able to work out how get a really clear recording of her visits, sooner or later – he was the cleverest person he knew, after all.

Of course, all this observation of the ghost had meant that he had stayed at home for much longer than his usual wont. Billie had been pleased, that went without saying, but he had to admit that he'd found her company more than normally annoying. She'd taken to insisting that she was seeing Mary all over the house: twice in the mirror on the upstairs landing, several times in the little panes of glass in the door of the main bedroom and even once in the huge gilt-framed affair above the fireplace in the grand sitting room. Dave shook his head. He'd specifically married Billie because she would be no intellectual challenge for him, and she'd been rightly swept off her feet by his brains and success. But this was definitely the downside. She was becoming a bag of nerves, and that was getting on *his* nerves. Stupid cow.

He sat back in his leather chair, and sipped his coffee, reviewing all the data that his array of costly devices had picked up overnight. His office sported several of the most expensive computers available, requiring a huge white polished desk to support their colossal and minimalist screens. He peered at the pages and pages of readings. It was interesting, lots and lots of information, but as of this moment he wasn't sure what it all meant. He could work it out, certainly he could, but to save himself some bother maybe he needed to borrow one of the firm's interns to do this grunt work. His mind drifted away into imagining that gorgeous redheaded girl from this year's intake coming here to do his bidding... In front of him, a single drop of clear water fell as if from nowhere and landed on the enormous high-resolution screen. It flickered and went dark.

'Shit!' Dave looked up and saw a huge, spreading stain on the stuccoed ceiling. A cloud of thick droplets gathered on its surface, and as he watched, plunged into the room below. 'No!' He sprang up and ineffectually ran about, wiping off water as it ran down the beautiful monitors, and then, as the rain began in earnest, jumping back out of the way as the electrics started to fizz alarmingly.

Dave backed out of the room, yelling for his wife. She'd left the fucking bath running, stupid, stupid bitch! He shouted and screamed for Billie, but she'd been heading into the garden when he'd last seen her and she couldn't hear him. Finally he stamped up the stairs, snorting with rage, and ran along the corridor to the bedroom suite to sort it out himself.

Their master bathroom was sumptuous, decked out in a suitably expensive rococo style. Dave cursed as he saw the reclaimed claw-footed bath was filled to the utter brim with shining water. The floor was soaked and he sloshed through ankle-deep to get to the taps and turn them off. He rolled up his sleeve and plunged his arm in up to the shoulder to unhook the plug, and the bath began rapidly emptying. He stood back, mentally rehearsing what he was going to be screaming at his wife when he found her in the garden. If she thought that just because –

The taps, beautiful, polished chrome taps, began to turn themselves on again. The plug, which he'd chucked on the side, jerked, and as he watched it slithered to the edge like some kind of landed fish, and plopped off into the water before swimming back to the gurgling hole and fitting itself back in. Dave stared. Then he leapt at the taps and struggled to turn them off again, but he couldn't, they were too strong… As he wrestled, he glanced down to the surface of the water which was rapidly filling the bath again, and he saw a face. For just a split second he thought it was his own reflection, but with a sickening jolt he realised that it was Mary's face, he recognised it, and it was smiling at him. Then two arms reached suddenly out of the water and pulled him under the surface. The grip was incredible, he couldn't free himself although he could feel his legs flailing, trying and failing to get a grip on the soaking floor. Dave struggled near the bottom of the bath, his eyes widening with horror as he saw the long chain floating from the plug lashing like a living thing. He tried to get away, but it wrapped itself around his throat and began to tighten, dragging him ever downward, despite his desperate attempts to get free. He was going to drown, he was going to drown and nobody was there to help him… and then he felt two hands gripping the back of his shirt and hauling him out. For a long second the pressure from the chain and from his rescuer pulled on him equally and he grit his teeth against the vicious bite of the cord of tiny steel balls that dug its fingers into his neck and refused to let him go. And then suddenly the plug burst out with a belch of suction and he was flying back out of the water and stumbling, arse-first, onto the sodden bathroom floor. Dave's fingers dug in and peeled the chain from around his throat and took a huge breath, most of which he coughed back up again, lying, exhausted, at his wife's feet. As his vision started to fade to black, he couldn't shake the amazement that she'd chosen to save him.

They finally managed to stop the flood by dint of turning off the water to the entire house from the stopcock by the kitchen, but by then the deluge had got into the main electrical circuits and fused the lot. Billie, still sodden, sent the bemused gardeners home early and tried to arrange for emergency plumbers and electricians, but it seemed the house's (or Dave's) reputation had gone before her and no-one was willing to come out before the following day. She finally accepted this, and climbed the wretched stairs again to break the news to her husband that they were going to have to rough it until the morning.

'Do you want to go to a hotel overnight?' she asked the rounded lump lying in their bed, covered with the duvet like a child hiding from a monster. The lump shook its head.

'Burglar alarm not working, not fucking leaving the place to be picked clean.'

'She nearly killed you, Dave!' shouted Billie, suddenly realising she was beyond the end of her tether, 'another minute and you would have bloody drowned!' He reluctantly pushed back the covers and sat up. She was shocked to see that he was looking his age for once, his years not being masked by a thick coating of overconfidence. A thin line of angry red dents ran around his throat.

'I know. I know!'

'I told you! I bloody told you she'd got out!' she repeated, rather unsympathetically.

'I can't... I don't...' Dave was almost whimpering. Billie shook him, hard.

'Pull yourself together! We've got to think, we've got to do something.' She glanced over her shoulder at the mirror on her dressing table. Had she seen something moving in it, just a moment before? Outside the bedroom window, the short autumn day was becoming gloomy. 'We need a priest.'

Dave had been shocked to be shaken by his wife, whom he almost didn't recognise in this furious-eyed woman. But the jolt had done its job, and he straightened up and swung his legs to the floor.

'No, no priests,' he didn't want this to get into the media, he must find a way to deal with it himself. 'There must be a way to – confine her back in the staircase. There must be a way, because she came with the fucking thing.'

Husband and wife stared at each other.

'But –' she said, standing, and Dave looked up at her. 'But maybe she had to get back into the staircase, because the rest of Warrington Hall burnt down. It was the only thing left.'

Rather typically, Dave declared that he wasn't leaving their bedroom, and so it was Billie who had to go and fetch what provisions she could find to help them survive the night. The house was dark, and she almost felt light-headed with terror as she picked her way slowly along the landing, guided only by the light on her phone. Its over-bright but narrow beam cast jagged shadows that jerked and jumped as she walked down the stairs, and the old wood creaked and moaned as she trod on each step. Was it giving her away or warning her? She couldn't decide.

She made it to the kitchen, and hurriedly dug out the heavy torch from the boot room, swinging it round the room and startling herself to see her own reflection, pale and terrified, springing into view across the blackness of the windows. She took a breath.

'Just be calm, just be calm,' she repeated, and fetched a bag which she began to fill with bottled water, bread, chocolate, apples, a pot of peanut butter… Digging in the cupboard under the sink she found some candles and matches which she slung in with a couple of saucers and then followed up with a handful of the sharpest knives from Dave's ridiculously expensive collection of chef's tools. Back along the pitch-black corridor she went, the darkness pressing down on the torch light. Was there someone here? Could she hear stealthy footsteps? The sound of breathing? That rustle, was that her or was it the sound of the Queen's stiff gown? Billie jerked the beam up and around, spinning to look behind her, hoping to catch – what? She didn't want to catch anything! She tried not to hurry but found herself getting faster and faster, until she was taking those damn stairs at almost a run and bursting into the bedroom so suddenly that Dave nearly wet himself.

'Christ!' his pale face drained of even more colour. 'What's the matter?'

She slammed the door, too out of breath to speak, but managed to shake her head. 'Nothing, it's ok,' but between them they dragged her heavy chest of drawers over the doorway. All the mirrors had been turned to the wall, or covered, and the curtains were closed, but as Dave and Billie lit the candles and placed them in the saucers about the room they saw a thousand tiny reflections, shiny polished surfaces and Billie had the crazy, disorientating thought that all these pinpricks were holes through into some greater reality, with them looking out – a pair of insects trapped under a colander, just waiting to be crushed. She shook her head and busied herself setting out their modest dinner.

The hours crawled by. When one of them need the bathroom they both went, despite having taken the door off its hinges and throwing the murderous bathplug out of the window. She'd never been so close to her husband, thought Billie, silently accompanying him back from a wee. How would they talk about this in the future? Would they laugh, or never mention it? Would it be a story about their resilience or an episode so shameful they tried to pretend it had never happened? A solid block of dread settled in her stomach; she knew in her soul that there would be no surviving this. Their time had come. She settled back in bed and realised that she felt quite calm. Let it all happen, she'd fought enough.

At about three o'clock Dave nodded off, slumped across the bedroom sofa. The sounds of his gentle snoring were quite soothing, and Billie was listening almost fondly to it when she realised she could also hear something else. Outside the golden orb of their candlelight the room was totally dark, but she could tell that somebody else was in here with them. She could feel their presence.

'Dave! Dave!' she hissed and then flew across the room and grabbed him. He woke with a jump, eyes wide and disorientated with fear. All of Billie's calm resolve dissolved in the white-hot terror that shot through her veins and she shouted: 'Go away! Go away! Leave us alone!' The candle flickered and blew gently out. They could both hear it now: the stealthy sound of a person moving. It was very, very quiet, just the slight creak of fabric and the scuff of a leather slipper…

In the morning, the electrician and the plumber banged on the door for fifteen minutes, laughing with each other about adding an even bigger charge to their call-out fees, before the housekeeper turned up and let them all in. She tried ringing her employers, but the calls went straight to voicemail. It was some time later before anyone thought of checking upstairs, and found the locked door with tell-tale traces of blackening around the frame. The fire brigade had a hard job breaking through - someone had put a heavy piece of furniture against it – and when they did the sight sent the tradesmen, who'd been crowding around on the landing, stumbling down the stairs to be sick.

'Death by misadventure,' ruled the coroner, who then went on to warn people about the risks of falling asleep with candles still lit.

'Double Death in Haunted House' screamed the tabloids.

James Rathie, who inherited the house under the terms of his business partner's will, decided against moving any of the expensive fixtures into his own properties, and had the building closed up. Frankly, the whole thing gave him the creeps.

And every night, at eleven o'clock, a woman in a dark blue dress walked calmly up the stairs, seen by no-one, but with a little smile upon her face.

THE BUCKLED SHOE

'I've come to see Tom', the nurse at the desk gave Andy a dubious look. 'I've got a letter from his mother, giving permission for me to see him.' He handed over the handwritten note, and she spent a long time examining it, as if to find a reason to ignore it. But Hilary's wishes were very clear: the staff were to allow him, Tom's oldest friend, to visit him at the private psychiatric hospital where he now resided.

'I'll have to get Dr Chambers,' she said at last, and left him sitting in the bland magnolia reception area for a long twenty minutes, before eventually returning and inviting him to go through a tall, Edwardian door into what he assumed was Dr Chambers' office. A greying man in a shirt and bow tie (no white coat, he noted) stood behind the desk, gazing out of the long window into the rhododendrons outside. He turned and they shook hands.

'Thank you for coming, Andy,' he said. 'I understand that you've been away?'

'Yes, I've been traveling in Australia.'

'You haven't been in touch with Tom recently?'

'He and I were in fairly regular contact by email until about three months ago. Then I unfortunately came off the worse in a car accident and was in hospital for seven weeks. During that time I had no access to anything other than a telephone, and apart from calls to my parents, that not much. By the time I had recovered enough to return home, and signed back into my email account, Tom was already here.' He shifted his weight slightly off his bad leg. 'What's been happening? I read his emails but...'

'Yes, his emails,' said the doctor, heavily. 'Well, Tom's mother has asked me to be honest with you. He's had a complete psychotic break, and despite our administration of appropriate medications he continues to experience delusions.' Chambers paused, and saw Andy's horrified expression. 'Do you know whether he was taking any drugs?'

'No, not that I know of,' he admitted. 'Why?'

'In this type of case, where the patient becomes so ill so quickly, an episode of drug taking often turns out to be the trigger.' He waved the young man out of the office and they went back into the corridor and through a secure, key-coded door. Beyond, the corridor, still bright, still magnolia, seemed different. It took Andy a moment to realise that everything was smoothed: no sharp corners, no ligature points. A long photomural of a beautiful garden in midsummer took up one wall, which seemed particularly cruel in this place of confinement.

Chambers paused outside a plain door. The younger man looked at him apprehensively.

'You'll have to take off your shoes,' said the psychiatrist.

Tom was sitting in a hospital chair, looking out of a window at the lawns outside. He rolled his head round to look at his old friend and faintly smiled.

'Hey, Tom,' said Andy, suddenly feeling stupid. He bit back a 'how are you' and instead went on: 'I've just got back from Australia. Your mum said you've not been too well.'

'I've gone round the bend, that's what everyone thinks.'

'What do you think?'

He was silent for a long moment and Andy felt crushingly sad, seeing at him in the old man's chair, thin and pale, and drugged to the eyeballs. His feet were bare, and looked cold.

'This is a mental hospital, isn't it?' he asked.

'Yeah. 'Fraid so, buddy.'

'Then maybe they're right, maybe I am crazy.' He seemed so lost, so tired. Then he snapped upright in his chair and glared at his friend. 'Did you read my emails?'

'When I left the hospital -' Andy began to explain, but Tom waved that away impatiently.

'But did you read them, read them all?'

'Most of them,' he didn't want to say that after the first couple he'd rung his friend's mother in alarm. Now Tom leaned forward and grabbed him tightly by the wrist. He was immensely strong, stronger than Andy ever remembered him being, and his eye flicked to the door.

Tom followed his glance, but then looked down at his friend's feet. Andy twitched his toes, self conscious about his mis-matching socks.

'They told you to take off your shoes, didn't they?' He nodded to himself. 'I can't bear shoes, shoes frighten me. Read my emails and you'll see why. Read the emails and go down to...' he swallowed a strange grimace - of fear, Andy realised. '...to the house and see what you think. An objective opinion. That's very scientific, isn't it? They'll like that here.' He let go of the other man's arm and sank back into the chair, all energy soaked away. 'You'd better go now'.

And feeing like a coward, Andy was pleased to be dismissed.

He didn't think his leg would be strong enough to ride the clutch for a couple of hours, so he borrowed his sister's automatic for the long drive down to the west country to visit Tom's cottage. It was getting late when Andy finally inched down the rubbly track that threaded through the gloomy and overgrown wood and up to the clearing where the house waited. He stopped the car, and turned off the engine to hear... nothing; perhaps it was the heaviness of an approaching storm that had silenced the birds. He got out and, turning on the spot, saw only old trees and ivy, a strip of grey sky, and the cottage itself. He couldn't have been more than half a mile from the nearest building but it felt like he was alone on the face of the earth.

Around and about, the signs of Tom's unfinished building work were clear - there was a stack of rotten floorboards by the back door, and near his feet lay a half-empty bag of cement, bloated and tumorous in the damp. Long tree trunks were buried in the scrubby grass, inexpertly cut from the ragged stumps that stood out everywhere like toadstools. Andy shook off a feeling of gloom, and walked over to peer in the windows. It was quite a small building, constructed out of large stones the colour of a purpling bruise. Inside it was black, not just dark, and gazing through the glass he had the stupid thought that someone could be standing in the room, looking back at him, and he wouldn't know. He spun on his heel and walked back to the car perhaps faster than he needed to. He climbed in, and pulled his tablet from the glove compartment to finally read Tom's emails.

1 May

Hey Andy! How's Australia?

I was going to say 'you lucky bastard', but I've had a brilliant bit of luck myself since you went. Guess what? I've bought a house! I know what you're going to say: WTF, you're too young, do you know what you're doing and all that. I've had all that crap off everyone else but I say sod it, it's a great place and dirt cheap, and I'm going to do it up and sell it. I've done my research and detached cottages make a mint around here. It's in a bit of a state but it was a probate sale, so what do you expect? Anyway, the deed is done and I collect the keys Monday. Going to camp in the building while I'm working on it, so that'll keep costs down. I am so excited and can't wait to get started! I'll send you some photos when I'm in.

Hope you're having a shit time in Oz, haha not really

See you

Tom

8th May

Alright? Haven't heard from you but I imagine you're Up Country or gone Walkabout or whatever you do. Let me know how you are, yeah?

Got the keys today and I've moved in!!! Fanfare, I am now officially a home owner! I reckon Gramps would have approved of me using my inheritance to do this, he always had an eye for a money-making opportunity. I thought of him today cos the house is full of stuff left behind by the old boy who used to live here. Proper granddad things like boxes of newspapers and tins of boot polish and a cut throat razor in the bathroom cupboard. Rusted to fuck it was, how he hadn't given himself tetanus over the years God only knows. Some of it might be worth keeping, but most of it is revolting or falling to pieces, or both. I'm going to have to get a skip.

I frightened myself half to death when I was clearing out the bedroom. There's one of those huge Victorian wardrobes jammed into the tiny room, and when I opened the door to check it was empty I thought I saw a man hanging from the rail. My heart nearly stopped beating with the shock, but then I saw that it was an old-fashioned suit with a hat balanced on the top. I've taken it out now and thrown it away, but it's put the idea in my head that Old Boy hanged himself in the house somewhere. Stupid, he probably died dribbling and senile in some old people's hell hole, but now I've thought of it I can't unthink it again. It's just the quiet here, it's getting on my nerves.

One more strange thing: he must have left a clock somewhere because I keep catching the sound of it ticking. I haven't found it yet so the Mystery of the Missing Clock continues!

Email me soon, you lazy bugger

T

19th May

Hey

Not sure if you're getting these emails, but it's nice to take a few minutes to sit down and write them, so I'm going to carry on. Just bin them if you're not interested.

Renovating a house is bloody hard work, and I am knackered. I think it's harder cos I'm doing it single handed, so as soon as you've got your arse back here I am rounding you up to help. Chaz and Oggy are going to come down later in the summer but for now it's just me. I did try having the radio blaring all day like a proper builder but the reception is terrible, it must be all the trees. Another thing on my never-ending to do list is to take a chain saw to the front garden and let some light in. I'm having to drive to Tescos just to get enough signal to send these emails!

Sorry, this is turning into a moan. I have actually done loads: two skips' worth of crap has been cleared out, the old kitchen has gone (100 years of grease, it took me days to get the smell of it off my hands), and I've taken down some stupid plasterboard partitions that Old Boy had put into the rooms upstairs to turn them into fuck knows what, rabbit hutches probably. I tell you, judging by the alterations he did, that guy was STRANGE. He'd even covered one of the windows with boards and papered over it. Why??? This is a cottage, so it's dark anyway, and he blocks off a whole window. And the rain's been getting in for fifty years and the whole frame and lintel has rotted to nothing.

The worst thing about it, though, was that a bird had got in at some point, and had died in there, trapped. I picked up the poor creature from all the leaves and dirt, and a whole shower of little brittle things fell out, and I realised they were dead flies, who'd got in after the bird but couldn't get out either. Their wings were still sparkling, even in all the dust.

I have never seen anything so horrible in my life.

Sorry to share this with you but I am trying to get it out of my head. That poor bird...

Right, have cracked open a beer and am feeling a bit more robust now.

It's an education, this building malarkey. I am spending all my time in the car park of the builder's merchants, looking on YouTube for how to repair stuff, before buying what I need to do it. And nobody will deliver to the house - not even takeaways!

When I've finished this I will be a proper builder, and no mistake. Still no sign of the clock.

Email me

T

22 May

Andy

I've attached some before and after pics... what do you reckon? And did you like the selfie?? That was me with a fucking chain saw, baby! I cleared nine trees from the 'garden' today and it is a bit brighter in the house. I was starting to blink when I went outside, like bloody Gollum or something so I just went and hired all the stuff and got it done. I'll chop it all up into firewood ready for the winter. Proper good fun and lots of NOISE. It's just too quiet here normally.

Mind you, as I'm sitting here in the sitting room typing this I can hear that bloody clock ticking again. I think it must be broken as I was in here earlier and there was no sound of it. Maybe something sets it off, a vibration from the road, maybe. It was probably those trees coming down, now I think about it. I am going to be stripping all the walls in here from tomorrow so I will find it. And then I'm going to stamp on it!

T

4 June

Hey mate

Starting to worry about you, are you ok? I've lost your mum's number else I'd ring and check. EMAIL ME.

Here's the latest episode of Tom's Fucking Weird House! I shouldn't say that, really. It makes it sound fun, which it isn't.

So you know that boarded up window I mentioned a while back? I had to replace the lintel (God bless YouTube) as it was completely rotten, and when I peeled back the paint and glue I found a wonky letter M carved into it. It must have been there for donkey's years, from the look of it, so I Googled it and it's apparently a witch mark!! Yes, a genuine sign to keep out witches and evil doers! I did try and save the carving to hang up as a curio but it just fell to bits. Maybe I should put a horseshoe over the window instead? Do you think that would work?

It's still not much lighter in here, despite felling all those trees. I can't understand it. It's like the dark in the house is cancelling out the light that's coming in. Or eating it up. Perhaps it's the ghost of the Old Boy who lived here. I shouldn't joke about that either.

Anyway, that's not even the weird part. You know I was stripping out the living room? I peeled it all back to the brick or stone (or wattle and daub in some places, can you believe it?) and there's no sign of that clock. But I can still hear it. It's much louder now, clearer somehow, a steady tick tick tick like a pulse or something. I even looked up the chimney in case OB in his wisdom had secreted it up there. I didn't find a clock, but I did find this leathery sort of bag that looked 500 years old. It was disgusting, some sort of mummified thing, but I couldn't bring myself to throw it away. Instead I drove down to the local museum and they told me it was a pig's heart!!! And worse than that it's apparently another anti-witch device, like the carving on the window. Blokey in the museum was delighted with it so I gave it to him, but now I'm wondering if that was a mistake. Do you think I should get another one and put it back up the chimney?

If you see a medicine man in Oz can you ask? Or is that the native Americans? Sorry, I'm a bit pissed tonight and typing distracts me a bit from listening to that bloody ticking.

Tom

5 June

Hey, it's three in the morning and I can't sleep. I'm camping in the biggest bedroom upstairs and that fucking wardrobe is just looming over me. I keep getting up and opening it, expecting to see that suit of clothes hanging there.

I did find it once, or it might have been a man. maybe that was a dream it's hard to tell

Tick tick tick goes the clock

Counting down to something

6 June

Andy

Sorry about the last email, I woke up this morning in the car, I must have driven somewhere to get the signal to send it. I can't remember where. Sorry, I think I'm losing it. How can you tell when something is real?

I'll send this and then head back. Perhaps I'll have a couple of days away from this place. Maybe when I've got the renovations on a bit further. T

8 June

Andy

I don't know what time it is in Australia but if you get this, can you email me back? My folks are away and I can't get hold of Oggy, and I am freaking out. PLEASE email me. Please.

There is something wrong with this house. I don't mean the shit plumbing and the wiring and all that, I mean that something is rotten here, something that is profoundly wrong. Like, wrong in a religious type way. God, this sounds insane and I don't know how to describe it. So I'll just tell you what's been happening.

This morning it absolutely poured with rain, hammered down. I was in one of the upstairs rooms, marking out where the plug sockets are going, and the water came streaming through the ceiling, so when it stopped I had to go into the attic to check the roof. I had been stupidly hoping the roof would be good enough, and I admit I didn't fancy going into the loft because I thought it would be too creepy! Which is a laugh because this whole place is creepy! So I told myself to grow up and got the head torch and a ladder, and squeezed through the loft hatch which is about the size of an A4 piece of paper.

Fortunately the roof space was empty (I was worried about yet more weird and non-wonderful possessions of OB) and I found the place where the rain was getting in and patched it up ahead of a proper fix at some future point. I was just about to head down again when I saw that someone had jammed a shoe into the corner between one of the rafters and the roof tiles. A shoe! I pulled it out, and it didn't want to come because the roof had sort of sagged on top of it, so it must have been there for a bloody long time. The shoe itself was very small, and had a buckle on the front, like something from a costume drama. It was really dry and old, but bent and shaped to someone's foot.

Anyway, I was going to bring it downstairs when it suddenly occurred to me that maybe this was another one of those witch things that the whole house seems littered with. That gave me a jolt, I can tell you, and I got really spooked stood there in that pitch-black attic with corners everywhere and just my little head torch to see with. I suddenly didn't want to be holding that shoe for another second and I quickly shoved it back into its spot by the rafter, but it didn't want to go in so I just crammed it onto the beam as best I could and practically ran back to the loft hatch and jumped down, slamming it behind me. I was still on the ladder, trying to stop myself having a panic attack, when I heard the shoe fall and hit the attic floor... I can't have wedged it in securely enough and the banging of the hatch must have jolted it loose. But I wasn't going back for it!!

I didn't think of it again for the rest of the day because I was decorating the living room (shame you can't get luminous paint as that room is so dark) and considering prying up the floorboards to find that fucking clock. It is so loud now! It ticks and it ticks and it ticks, and you don't notice you're hearing it until you realise you've been listening to it for ages. It must be under the floor or something because I can hear it in the kitchen as well now. And then that makes me think of that creepy Edgar Allan Poe story and that really doesn't help.

After an hour or two I realised I'd left some masking tape upstairs and I needed it, so I went up the little dark staircase and fetched it from the back bedroom. I was just about to go down again when I heard something from above my head.

I shit you not, Andy, it was a footstep.

I completely froze. And then I heard it again, a distinct step, exactly like someone walking on the attic floor. There was a pause, and another step. And then my ears seemed to tune up and I realised that there was another sound, in between the steps - a dragging sound. It went step drag step, step drag step, like a person who had a limp, or someone with only one shoe...

I was down the stairs and outside and in my car reversing up the drive before you could say go. I didn't stop till I'd got to the nearest little town and I'm lucky I didn't get a speeding ticket on the way. I'm sitting here in a coffee shop now, emailing this, and waiting for my heart to stop hammering so I can go back and find out what's going on.

Because there's something wrong there, Andy. I think I've let something out, or let something in, or someone. I know this doesn't make any sense but it's the feeling there, like I'm the one who shouldn't be there, like precautions are being taken to get rid of ME.

I don't want to go back but I've got to find out.
I'll let you know
Your friend, Tom

Andy looked up from the tablet screen and the day outside had dwindled to nothing. Mist and darkness hung from the trees in glutinous sheets, and the house, Tom's house, sat in its little clearing and seemed to watch him. A light flicked on in an upstairs window, and then went out. Could someone be there? He'd been so engrossed in reading the emails that perhaps he hadn't seen a person slip by the car in the gloom. Andy sat and chewed his lip for a minute, and then grabbed his mobile and got out.

He really didn't want to go into the house. His feet were literally dragging. He mentally shook himself - was he a bloody baby? For some reason the sounds and smells of his car accident were loud in his mind: the scream of distorting metal, the reek of spilling petrol... He shoved the memories away and turned the handle of the door.

Inside, it was black dark, breathless, waiting. He snapped the light switch but nothing happened, and his fingers fumbled the torch app before it came on suddenly in a blaze of white light. Andy blinked it out of his eyes and shone the beam around, picking out the shapes of furniture under sheets, a box of tools abandoned on the floor, a huge stone fireplace like a black maw. Moving reluctantly inside he felt the silence as a tangible thing, a heaviness. But there - he hesitated, head cocked, listening. Yes, there was a clock ticking somewhere.

He stopped at the bottom of the stairs and looked up. All was in darkness now. Could he feel someone up there, waiting? And then there was a creak, the betrayal of old floorboards, and a step. A pause, then another step.

'Who's up there?' The young man shouted, and gritting his teeth against the urge to run, he clambered with difficulty up the narrow staircase, the phone's white light bobbing madly on walls and steps, dazzling him and throwing shadows everywhere. He rounded the banister and headed down to a room where now yellow lamplight picked out the edges of the door. Andy heard the screaming of the tires and smelled the fuel, and the dark landing canted fiercely. He fought on and burst inside.

There was a bare bulb hanging from the low ceiling, a window showing black with his own frightened reflection painted on it, and Tom. Andy stared. Tom was standing, barefoot, head down, under the small, closed hatch into the attic. Slowly, he looked up and fixed the other man with a look of complete despair.

'Tom! How...?' began his friend, but then the phone, held forgotten in his hand, began to ring. The sound was obscenely loud in this place. In his haste to silence it, Andy pressed the answer button and a voice rang out:

'Andy, it's Oggy. Mate, it's Tom, he's...' The sound faded away and the phone went dead. In horror, Andy watched his friend slowly look up as the sound of a step crunched onto the ceiling, and then another. Above his head, the loft hatch grated and began to move.

SWEETIE

I first saw the ghost on a Tuesday morning, as I was slumped in my seat on the number 215 heading into town. It was a hot, grey, airless summer day and I wasn't looking forward to a whole eight hours of shelving in the College library. But a job was a job, and I was saving cash (and collecting funny stories) for when I was back at Uni in two months. The bus wasn't full, just me and a scattering of elderly people heading off for a morning's shopping. On a whim I'd sat in a different spot today, and outside the window a whole new strip of shops and pavements and cars and houses and trees unfurled as we slowly made our way into the town centre. I like looking at things through the windows of buses and trains, and so I ignored the book, open in my lap, and just watched the world literally go by.

We had got as far as a row of small shops near two or three schools when the traffic lights held us up. I examined the dusty antiques shop on the corner with its dark and mysterious window, and the gaudy estate agents, and a very pink shop which seemed to be selling very pink things to small girls (or to their mothers). And then I looked at the old-fashioned sweet shop that sat in the middle of the run. It had oversized jars of stripy humbugs and bright yellow lemon drops, and sparkly rhubarbs and custards, and curls of black liquorice. Just looking at it all made my mouth water, and I fleetingly wondered if the red light would hold long enough for me to jump out and buy a quarter of something. The sun broke free of its bodyguard of clouds just at that moment, and dazzled me, and when I put my hand down from shielding my eyes I saw that there was a very stout old lady standing in front of the sweetshop. A very stout old dog stood by her side, and as I watched, the woman dipped her hand into a small, white paper bag and held out a toffee, which the dog sniffed with keen interest and then took gently from her fingers.

The bus suddenly gave a hiss and a jolt and started to move away, and as I turned my head to keep the old lady and her dog in sight they simply snapped out of view. I blinked. I craned my head to look back, startling the old man sitting behind me, but I couldn't see them. I swivelled in my seat to try and catch a glimpse of the lady's grey mackintosh through the bus' back window - straining to see past the heads of the passengers sitting on the back seat – but I was too late. I sat down again and ignored everyone looking at me, and instead tried to review what it was I had actually seen. I played it again in my mind: old lady, dog, the gift of a toffee, and then – nothing. It was as if they had only been visible from the front, and now my perspective had changed, they'd vanished, like looking at a rainbow from the wrong angle. I frowned and shook my head. What a load of rubbish I was thinking.

The following morning I sat on the right hand side of the bus again. I couldn't help it –

my legs just walked me there automatically. Again we rattled and huffed our way into town, and my nose was practically pressed to the window when we began to approach the little row of shops. Agonisingly we lurched and stopped, lurched and stopped, getting closer to the sweetshop but still too far to make out any figures standing outside it. Then the bus put on a bit of a spurt and for a second we were exactly alongside and I saw the stout old lady and her stout old dog, and the white paper bag and I was looking for the toffee when the traffic spontaneously cleared and we pulled away. Again, the figures of the woman and her pet slipped into nothing, like something turning sideways and disappearing through – what? A crack in reality? I flopped back, playing again and again the moment when I'd almost seen them edge-on, like cut-out puppets in a paper theatre. There was something fundamentally wrong about it all, and I shuddered in my cool summer dress, the green vinyl of the bus seat cold against my legs.

Later that morning, Mrs Collins sought me out where I was sitting on the floor, pretending to shelve a series of extremely boring volumes of Statutory Instruments. The big, floppy, cream booklets were spread out all around me in a fan, and I wasn't looking at them but instead was staring into the dark space on the bottom shelf that they had vacated. My mind's eye was reviewing a bright street and a sweetshop and the old lady and her dog turning from three dimensions into one, and then none.

'Jo!' I jumped guiltily. The kind face of the Deputy Librarian was wearing her sternest expression, which wasn't very stern but made me feel bad anyway. 'What are you doing? I was expecting you downstairs half and hour ago to help me with moving those shelves.'

I hastily began shoving government publications into their bindings. 'Sorry, Mrs Collins.'

She stood and looked at me for a minute, and then pulled over a kickstep stool with a practised flip of her sandaled foot and sat down on it. Perched there in her ballooning taupe jumper and skirt she reminded me of a benign mushroom.

'What's the matter?' she asked simply. 'This isn't like you, I never have to chase you! You're my reliable girl!'

I smiled. We got on, Mrs Collins and I, and she frequently lamented that Ed and Claudia, the other two summer interns, were more interested in groping each other in the stacks than in doing any actual work.

'Sorry,' I said again. 'Something's just put me off my stride this morning.' I flapped a Statutory Instrument lamely.

'What sort of something? Somebody been rude to you? Was it Irene?'

I smiled and shook my head. The library's resident Rude Old Lady had been quite nice to me lately, and had actually smiled this morning when I'd brought up the latest obscure tome she'd requested from the basement storage area. 'No, it's –' suddenly the words came out in a rush. 'I saw something, on the way to work, and it doesn't make any sense. It was really… disturbing. And I can't get it out of my head.' I didn't dare say the word 'ghosts'; plain and practical Mrs Collins would think I had totally lost it.

'Oh dear! Was it a crime or something?' her eyes were wide with alarm. I hastily shook my head.

'No! No, nothing like that.'

Reassured, she sat back and regarded me. She blinked a little as she thought it over. 'Could you get more information?' she asked, at last.

'What do you mean?'

'Well, you said that what you saw didn't make sense. That suggests to me that you don't have all the facts. Could you collect more data?'

'Er…' Could I? 'I suppose I could take a closer look…' Maybe if I got off the bus then I'd have more time to observe the woman and the dog, and then perhaps I'd see that there wasn't a mystery after all. I smiled up at the librarian's kindly face. 'Yes, I can see how I can get another perspective on this, and that might very well help. Thank you!'

Mrs Collins hid her pleased smile by bustling herself to her feet. 'Good. One problem solved! Now come and have a cup of tea and help me with these bally shelves.'

Naturally, the next morning the bus was late. Not just five minutes, but twenty five whole minutes late. I was in agonies at the bus stop, hopping into the traffic every few minutes to peer hopefully down the road, and by the time it eventually arrived I was stressed and panicked and worrying about being late to work as well as everything else. I chewed my lip with anxiety all the way down the hill and through the new housing estate, and I kept telling myself that perhaps I would still see the old lady and her dog despite it being a different time of day, but we sailed past the sweetshop and the pavement in front was just empty. I slumped. It seemed that I'd missed the slot for whatever magic or singularity or break in the space time continuum or whatever it was, and there was to be no performance today.

Just to add to my bad mood, Mrs Collins

had called in to say that her elderly mother had taken a fall and she was waiting with her at the hospital to get checked out, and that meant that all morning I was put onto Mr Andrews' team in the medical library. Mr Andrews was a tall, ginger, emaciated man who was permanently irritated at the summer staff, as if prepared in advance for our inevitable stupidity and annoyingness. He gave me a trolley overflowing with returned books and just pointed at the reading room, and so I spent an unpleasant few hours shelving things like *The Colour Encyclopaedia of Eye Diseases* and *Surgical Techniques in Dentistry* whilst trying not to look at the covers. By the time lunch came I was as bad tempered as my boss, and had a crick in my neck.

The staff room seemed especially noisy today, and crowded too. I jammed onto a bench next to Mr Javed from Psychology, and found I was sat opposite the dreaded Claudia and Ed who appeared to be crammed onto the same chair. The racket and the crush and the nauseating display from across the table all made me want to scream, so I wolfed my limp, home-made sandwich and then slipped into the gloom and quiet of the newspaper archive to read my book undisturbed for the remainder of my break. Hardly anyone ever consulted the bound copies of yellowing papers anymore, so I was surprised to see that one of the huge volumes was already out, laid open on the wide reading table at an issue from about ten years before. I have never been able to resist reading any words in front of me – whether on a cereal packet, a label, a road sign or a book – and so I automatically moved across and looked at the open page.

ELDERLY WOMAN DIES IN HOUSE FIRE screamed the headline under a photo of a blackened building with forensics vans drawn up outside. I read on.

Police say a body has been found at the scene of a fire that swept through the home of Sylvia Grayling, aged 84, in Hadlow Terrace on Tuesday. Although formal identification is still in progress, neighbours confirmed that Miss Grayling lived alone, and a police spokesman has stated that they believe the remains to be those of the missing pensioner. The cause of the house fire is still under investigation, but fire brigade sources indicated that faulty wiring may have been to blame. MORE ON PAGE FOUR.

Obediently, feeling remote and dreamlike, I turned to page four. And there was a photo of the lady from the sweetshop.

I rode home that evening deep in thought. I'd learned from the newspaper that Miss Grayling had been unmarried, and had lived all her life in the little house in Hadlow Terrace, which was about two streets away from the sweetshop. Aside from the headline and the article about the fire, there had been just one more piece in the paper noting her funeral, with the comment that it had been 'sparsely attended'. It seemed that nobody had really known Sylvia, and when the sensation of her death had worn thin, nobody had really been interested in her either. She could have been any generic old lady, seen going about her business every day in her mack and her headscarf, but who 'kept herself to herself'.

Only one neighbour had made any kind of personal observation about her, saying that she'd been very upset when her dog had died some months before. I sat on the jolting bus and felt the whole thing to be deeply sad.

I didn't know who had left the paper open at that page, as when I'd asked at the front desk the duty librarian didn't think she'd seen anyone using the newspaper archive that morning. I told her that someone had left a volume of the local paper out, and she had just laughed and said it must have been the library ghost, which hadn't been a helpful comment, I felt. But whoever it had been, now I did indeed have some of the extra information that Mrs Collins had suggested I find; I knew the old lady's name, and how she'd died, and I knew that nobody had really paid any attention to her. But I'd seen her, and I was paying attention.

In the morning, the bus driver looked at me as if I was crazy when I rang the bell and stood by the doors waiting for it to pull up at the stop before the sweetshop.

'You want to get out here, love?' he asked, having seen me trundling all the way into town every day for the past four weeks. 'You sure?' I just nodded. I was too nervous to speak, and so pretty much ignored his kindness and hopped out onto the pavement as soon as the doors were opened. As the bus pulled away, I saw the driver's puzzled expression was mirrored on the faces of every other passenger, who all stared at me from their windows as I stood by the stop. And then it was gone, and I walked up the street to the point outside a wine bar that I judged was exactly opposite the sweetshop. My heart was banging in my chest, and I gripped the strap of my satchel tightly, and then I turned to look across the road.

There she was.

The stout old lady was belted tightly into her mackintosh, that looked as if it had once been beige but had faded to dishwater grey. Her headscarf was greenish, again showing signs of wear, and she was bending over to offer the sweet to the stout old dog who was slowly wagging his tail in happy anticipation of his treat. I glanced quickly to either side to judge the traffic, and then walked across the road. They didn't disappear, or change, but continued what appeared to be almost a conversation without paying any attention to what was happening around them. I stepped onto the brick pavement and waited a second to let a man in headphones walk past me. Nobody was giving the woman and her dog a second glance.

'Miss Grayling? Sylvia?' my voice sounded pathetically quavery. I cleared my throat and tried again. 'Um, may I speak to you?'

For a moment I wasn't sure whether she heard me, and in fact whether she could hear me or was just on some kind of time loop or – then she turned and looked at me. I caught my breath. She frowned slightly as if puzzled and then said: 'Yes?'

'Hi, I'm Jo,' I had thought hard about whether to offer my hand and in the end had been frightened in case she took it and it felt *dead*. So I tightened my grip on my bag and tried to smile. I smiled at Sylvia and then I turned and smiled at her dog. It looked at me out of benevolent brown eyes and gave its tail a wag. 'I've seen you from the bus, over the past few days, and I just thought I'd, er, get out and say hello.'

She looked so completely real, standing there in her coat and scarf, the white paper bag of toffees held in her knuckly hand, that I suddenly felt hugely embarrassed. Perhaps I'd imagined the vanishing bit and this was just a completely ordinary old lady on her way to the shops. I felt my cheeks go hot and red.

'Hello,' said the woman, her eyes ranging over me as if taking me all in. 'Not many people see us, and I think you're the first to come up to speak to us.' She and the dog shared a glance that seemed full of unspoken communication. 'This is a bit of a surprise.' Her watery blue eyes were very piercing, I noticed.

'What's the name of your dog?' I asked, and then Miss Grayling's face broke into a smile that shone in her pale face. I smiled back, and again smiled at the dog. His wide old head was turned and he was gazing at his mistress with pure love in his big eyes.

'Sweetie, that's his name,' she said, beaming at him and then at me. 'I called him Sweetie because he was always such a sweetheart, even when he was a puppy. He never chewed anything or caused me any bother, he was just a love. And he's always loved his sweets, haven't you?'

I tentatively held out my hand to him, and he sniffed in my direction but didn't really move, just settled his thick paws and swung his tail.

'He does seem very sweet.' I said. There was an awkward pause, and I felt at once the complete absurdity of this situation. I almost laughed at it. 'I'm so sorry,' I said, 'for interrupting you, but I just wanted to…' What on earth had I been trying to do? '…see if you were alright.'

Sylvia straightened up and pushed the bulging paper bag into her coat pocket. 'That's very kind of you, dear. And yes, we're alright, aren't we, Sweets?' At the mention of his name, the dog huffed happily. 'You're lucky to have caught us, actually, because we're off tomorrow, somewhere new. They never let us stay in one place too long.'

'Who don't?'

'Them, the –' a lorry thundered past and I couldn't hear what she was saying, but she was pointing emphatically down towards the pavement. '-every week or so we have to move, don't want to let us get settled, I suppose.' She must have seen my look of confusion. 'It wasn't an accident, you see, the fire. I did in on purpose. Sweetie had gone, after fourteen years he had gone, and I couldn't bear it, just couldn't bear it without him.' Her eyes went distant as she remembered. 'Nobody understood. He's just a dog, they said, just a dog, buck up now. They didn't see how much he meant to me.' She set her mouth in a bitter line. 'As if it didn't matter, that he was dead, as if I could just forget him and carry on.' She fell silent, and the dog very gently licked her hand.

'That was a horrible thing for people to say,' I said.

'Yes, yes, it was.' She nodded at me. 'The doctor even suggested I buy another dog! Huh!

There was ever only one Sweetie.' She smiled at her friend. 'I never married, you see, and to be quite truthful I find people very irritating. But not Sweetie. He was all the company I ever wanted, always so happy to see me, and interested in what I was doing… When he died, well, I couldn't go on. What was the point?'

'And the fire?'

She grinned then, and I saw what she'd looked like when she'd been a child and then a young woman and then a lady with her own life, and before she'd become that pitiable old woman mourning the loss of her dog. 'I lit a candle and left the gas on! Why not, go out with a bang, that's what I thought! Hah!' She gave a short chuckle. 'But it was suicide, you see, there's no getting away from that. And if you break the rules then you have to put up with the consequences.'

'Consequences?' I began to ask, but she cut me off.

'Anyway, we're together again, aren't we? That's the only important thing.' Dog and woman laughed at each other with simple happiness, and she began tightening the belt on her coat. 'And we must be off; no rest for the wicked. Thank you for stopping to talk to us today.'

She smiled, and as I smiled back I saw that all around the edge of her she was starting to fray, wearing away like the fabric on an old armchair, revealing the background of the street and the shop behind her. Then she was all transparent, a shadow of light, or a blotch on the eye, in the vague shape of an old lady and an old dog.

'Take care!' I called urgently, but she had already gone, and a woman pushing a buggy through the space where Sylvia and Sweetie had been standing gave me a frown and a funny look. I turned away, not wanting anyone to see I had tears rolling down my face, and put my hand into my satchel to find a tissue, but instead I pulled out a small, white paper bag that bulged with toffees.

MINE

Polly drew up outside the large, white house and looked at it doubtfully through the rainy windscreen. It had been a frustrating journey – her last house-sit had been on the other side of the country and to get here she'd had a long drive along motorways choked with post-holiday traffic. Ordinarily, the agency tried to arrange things to reduce the amount of travelling between assignments, but she'd been called in as a last minute replacement and had had to put up with the aggravation this caused.

The house had a closed look. Its windows were dull, and reflected the lowering grey sky that was pouring rain down on the empty garden and drumming onto the roof of her car. It had been repainted sometime recently, Polly's experienced eye told her, but somehow this hadn't stopped the building from exuding a feeling of abandonment. She shook herself. Why was she still sitting in the car? She needed to get inside, get organised, and unpack – rain or no rain. She opened the door and then ran round to the boot of her little Renault, and hauled out her suitcase and laptop bag, and a carrier bag of basic provisions. By the time she'd staggered the few feet to the front porch she was soaked, and freezing.

'Bloody stupid weather for August,' she said to herself, and shook the bunch of keys she'd been couriered to find the right one. The door opened slowly - reluctantly, she found herself thinking – and inside, the hall was dark and unwelcoming. A strange sensation crept through Polly's stomach and up her spine; she felt like she was intruding. But she knew nobody was here. That's why the owners had contracted the house-sitting company in the first place. She wiped the rain from her face and stepped resolutely over the threshold.

She dumped her cases by the stairs and switched on the lights. They were yellowed and feeble, showing up the shadows in the corners, and highlighting the forbidding array of closed doors that faced her. Polly picked one and found it opened into a largeish kitchen, very old fashioned, but fortunately clean and tidy. She hated starting a house-sit by cleaning up other people's grime. The window overlooked the back garden, which, like the one at the front, had a mowed lawn and absolutely nothing else in it. Although it was only half past six, darkness was gathering so Polly turned on the strip light overhead and pulled down the blind, which turned out to have a strange pattern of birds and flowers on it that looked like something from another planet. It gave her the creeps. She turned quickly away and went to the kettle, emptying out the dregs of water inside and refilling it from the tap. She turned it on and the familiar hissing sound of boiling made her feel better.

'I've got the spooks,' she said out loud, and half-laughed to herself. Polly usually house-sat for people going on holiday who wanted someone to look after their pets while they were away. She liked animals, and as well as all the usual ones had been called upon to care for parakeets, parrots, rabbits, and even reptiles. She decided that this strange feeling was her just missing the hopeful faces and welcoming eyes of the family dog or cat, who would normally follow her about as she settled herself in. Here, there were no animals to look after. The kettle, clattering to a boil, clicked off, leaving a heavy silence. She suddenly decided to leave the tea for now, and finish looking around the house. 'The sooner I get it over with, the better,' she found herself thinking.

A doorway from the kitchen led into the darkened living room, where she could just pick out the heavy shapes of furniture in the gloom. She couldn't find the light switch, so steeled herself to walk across the space to the opposite door, and turn on the ceiling lamp from there. She flicked the switch and spun round, having that horrible feeling that somebody was standing right behind her – but there was no-one, just a wing backed chair that was sitting at an angle to the fireplace and which seemed to be looking right at her. The back was stained, as if from years and years of somebody's head resting on it, and to the side was a little table with an ashtray and a box of matches on it. Polly got a sudden mental picture of an old woman with grey hair, sitting in that chair and smoking cigarette after cigarette, half turned away from the gas fire and the television, and looking up all the time towards the door where she, now, stood.

'God's sake,' she whispered to herself and stamped loudly out of the room and up the stairs. The long drive must have tired her out, she thought, marching into each of the bedrooms. The largest had a bed that was made up under a peppermint green coverlet, and which had hairbrushes laid out neatly on the dressing table as if waiting for their owner to return. She backed out of this room hurriedly, and looked into the room next door, which was alarmingly filled with junk: old toys with shining glass eyes, broken chairs, stacks of sagging boxes and piles of mouldering fabric that smelt of decay. Fortunately, the tiny spare room at the back of the house was just empty, and so she unpacked her case and swiftly put her own duvet and sheets on the stripped bed. Debbie from the agency had warned her to bring her own things, as no-one had been living in the house for some time and the owner was abroad. Polly felt better when she saw the cheerful yellow and white pattern spread out. It clashed horribly with the vivid orange curtains and the treacle-tart carpet, but she didn't mind that.

She took her washbag and towel into the peach coloured bathroom, and forced herself to open the mirrored cabinet to check what might be inside, expecting old pill bottles and used tubes of toothpaste. At first sight it was empty, and she was half-way through a sigh of relief when she noticed a smeary glass stood on the top shelf in one corner. Hesitantly she fetched it down, and held it up to the overhead light to see through the murky water inside. The movement swirled the contents and a pair of false teeth swam into view, grotesquely distorted by the heavy glass, each tooth yellowed and nicotine-stained. With a shudder of disgust Polly shoved the glass back onto the shelf and slammed the cupboard door shut. As it closed, for a split second it reflected the landing and Polly jumped at the figure of an old woman standing in the doorway to the room with the green bed. She spun round, hands gripping the sink, but there was nobody there.

'Shit!'

Her heart was hammering in her chest, and there was a roaring in her ears that she thought was her blood pounding through her veins, but then Polly realised it was the sound of the kettle boiling in the kitchen below her.

She ran down the stairs trying not to look back up to the door of the green bedroom, and made it into the kitchen just to see the button on the back of the old-fashioned kettle snap off. She frowned at it; she was sure it had turned itself off before she'd gone up. The thought of upstairs made her stomach turn over – had she really seen the old woman? Was it a – she couldn't bring herself to say the word, even in her own mind. No, she refused to accept that.

This was just a creepy old house, a creepy old un-lived in house, she corrected herself, and she was imagining things. She dug out her phone and rang the office.

'Thank you for calling Mi Casa House Sitters,' intoned Debbie's voice on the answering machine. Polly rolled her eyes. 'There's nobody available to take your call at the moment, so please leave a message after the tone.'

Beep!

'Debs, it's Polly Hammond,' she stared at the psychedelic window blind until it made her eyes blur, then turned round. 'I'm at that house in Bentham, and I wanted to go over the brief again. This is a different set-up to what I expected,' she went on, drily, 'and I'm not sure it's going to suit me. You know my number, please call.'

She ended the message and sighed. There would be no answer from the office tonight, but perhaps Debbie would ring in the morning. At least that little touch of the outside world had calmed her down, and reminded her that she could just walk out of the front door, if she wanted to. Nobody was keeping her here.

That decided, Polly fetched the carrier bag of food from the hallway and began making herself some supper. She wasn't a big eater, and certainly didn't have much of an appetite tonight, but routine was important when you led as nomadic existence as she did, and the actions of heating a tin of soup and cutting some bread were calming. She carried her tray into the sitting room with her head up, bravely, and turned on the big old television in the corner. It came on, after a worrying second, and she sat on the sofa and ate her minestrone while watching news of a civil war in some far-off place of yellow dust and glaring sunlight that looked as different from this rainy corner of Oxfordshire as she could imagine. Feeling a bit more herself, Polly went back to the kitchen and washed up, then switched on the kettle again for a cup of tea. She stood over it while it rattled and boiled (breaking the cardinal rule of watching the pot) and as she was stirring the teabag in the mug she thought that it was probably just faulty, and had turned itself on randomly while she was upstairs. She'd have to buy a cheap new one tomorrow, and charge it back to expenses.

Tea made, she went back into the sitting room and changed channels onto some antiques programme while she set up her laptop on the coffee table. She entered her password and was reflecting that she was going to have to use her mobile account to access her email when she became aware that she could smell smoke. She looked up, and in the ashtray next to the wingback chair she saw a long, white cigarette. It had burned down a little way, and a clear curl of grey smoke was rising from the red tip and disappearing into the gloom near the ceiling. Polly stared at it. She was frozen, half-hunched over the laptop, and from this awkward position she slowly turned her head and looked towards the tall chair. It was empty.

Dreamlike, she pushed the computer away and stood up, crossing the room in a stride and picking up the cigarette. It was a completely ordinary fag, the paper smooth, the filter orange

– but with a smear of darkish lipstick on it. Polly flung it away from her and it landed in the ashtray, and then she grabbed it and stabbed it out, violently, until it was broken and twisted and cold. She spun round, eyes wildly sweeping from side to side. There was someone else in the house! Some old woman was in here, those were her things upstairs, and she'd been in here and lit her ciggie whilst Polly was in the kitchen. She was so furious, that bloody agency had sent her to a house where someone was already living.

'Who's there?' she shouted, and then louder: 'Who is it? Come out! I know you're in here!'

'Who are *you*?' said a voice from behind her, and Polly whirled round to stare at the figure of an old woman, who was sitting calmly in the armchair, smoking a long white cigarette. 'This is my house. *Mine*.'

Polly stared and could feel her eyes bulging. It was the same woman from the green room upstairs. She was tall, with frizzy grey hair and dark eyes that were narrowed and cold.

Her mouth was drawn in a disapproving scowl, a mere line of dark lipstick, and the hand holding the cigarette tapped the arm of the chair impatiently, but when Polly's eyes travelled down the woman's swollen legs they tapered away and dissolved into nothing, as if she was a badly-cropped photograph.

'Who –' whispered Polly.

She tried to understand what was going on, but her brain wouldn't function, and a white moth of fear was beating in her throat and around her heart. The old woman smiled, and Polly took a step backwards, bumping into the coffee table.

'Mine.' The ghost of the old woman sat up and stubbed out her cigarette. Behind her, the television switched itself off, the picture disappearing into a single white dot, and then blackness. The lights in the hall, and then the kitchen and the sitting room turned themselves off, one by one, leaving only a small lamp by the old woman's chair. Polly tried to get away, but fell back over the low table, sprawling back onto the patterned carpet, while the woman rose from her seat and took a step forward on her half-formed legs, smiling down at her with mirthless eyes. She stooped, and Polly felt a cold, white pain in the centre of her chest as the old woman jabbed her with a pale finger. She blew out a long cloud of cigarette smoke into Polly's face, everything around the edges of the room began to fade, letting darkness swirl in.

'Now you're mine too,' she said.

THE UNDERTAKERS

I had been up all night, staring at the computer screen. Letter by painful letter, I'd pecked out the content of the email that I was finally sending to Charlotte, all those miles away. Each full stop felt like a tiny nail in the coffin of our relationship, and by the time I'd pressed 'send', I was drained and spent, a bloodless husk, all hope sucked out of me. And so ended five years of my life. I looked at the clock: three thirty a.m. The window was a reflecting square of black, catching me pale and pensive, seated at the desk I'd probably been sitting at too long during those five years. On impulse I jumped up, grabbed my jacket, and left the flat.

Three thirty is a time when the world is dead. The night has crystallised the city into silence, and the morning seems nothing more than a cruel dream that will never come true. I walked down the wide, empty pavements, stepping in and out of the cones of orange sodium light, and shoved my hands into my pockets. What a pointless waste everything was. Without Charlotte, what was I going to do now?

Inevitably, the bright square of light from the window of the all-night caff drew me in. I stopped outside its steamy glass, and then pushed open the door and blinked at the fluorescents for a second before walking up the counter. A tired woman in an apron waved me away.

'Just sit down, love. I'll be over in a sec.'

I sat at a yellow-topped table facing the window, and when the waitress shambled over, ordered tea and toast. She nodded, and shuffled off to speak to an unseen figure in the kitchen.

'Can I tell you something?' the voice, almost in my ear, made me jump out of my chair. I swivelled round and saw a small man leaning across from the next table.

'Shit!' I glared at him, and he smiled apologetically, but made no move to back away. 'What is it?'

'Sorry, it just seems to good a chance to pass up, if you don't mind.'

The woman wandered over with my mug and plate of buttery toast, and didn't cast a glance at my neighbour. I took a sip, burnt my tongue, and relented a bit.

'What's the problem?' The man shuffled his chair over to mine, and smiled again. I looked at him properly. He had seemed small, but now I saw he was just stooped, and that and the tightly-buttoned black overcoat and heavy scarf gave him a curiously old-fashioned air. He eyed my toast and licked his lips. 'Want some?' I offered.

His face quirked into a broader smile, and he shook his head. 'If you would be so good, my friend, as to hear my story?' he asked, and I saw a flash of something in his eyes that I couldn't place. Was it anxiety? Or humour? Either way, the warmth of the café and the comfort of the food had combined to make me relax. Let him talk. What could be the harm? I thought.

'Go on, then.' I said.

He shuffled a bit closer again and a scent of mothballs and something rank fluttered into my nose, quenching my appetite at a stroke. But he was speaking now, and there was no stopping him.

'My name, sir, is Malcolm Raymond Robinson.' If he'd been wearing a hat, he'd have doffed it, I thought, mentally shaking my head. 'I'm from just up the road, lived there all my life. I work in a shop, a hardware shop, nails and buckets, you know the sort of gear. Not a very adventurous person, perhaps, just a regular type of chap – read the paper, do the garden, like a pint occasionally.' He drew breath, his gaze turning inward, caught in his own story. 'About two weeks ago I was walking home from the pub, I'd had a few,' he threw me a glance, 'but I wasn't too bad and my feet know the way, alright, so I know I was on my street. But as I came up to my house I thought I'd got lost after all because there was an undertaker's carriage parked outside the door.' I turned my head. 'You know, one of those old-fashioned ones with black horses with feathers on their heads,' his pale hand twirled above his own bald crown in emphatic description. I nodded, and he carried on. 'Well, as you can suppose I thought something terrible had happened while I was out, that my wife or my children had...' He swallowed. 'But then everyone knows I drink in the Red Lion and someone would have run to tell me, I was sure. Anyway, I hurried over and then I saw there was an undertaker sitting up at the front.

"What's going on?" I asked him, all out of breath, *"Who has died?"*

He looked at me, and a coldness spread all the way through me, a coldness and a great feeling of —' he selected his words, 'desolation. Like there was no light, no hope, not anymore. I told myself it was simple fear, that's all, and looked up at the man for his answer. He seemed very tall, sat up there, and the horses were standing very quiet, like, not stamping their feet or anything.'

'What did he say?' I couldn't help but ask the question. He nodded at me, as if this was the right thing to do.

'He looked down at me, from all the way up there, and he said: *"We've come a little early, sir, just a little early,"* and with that he flicked the reigns and those silent horses sprang into motion, and they was off down the street and round the corner before I could say knife.' The little man shook his head, and leaned in, voice dropping. I was faintly aware of the hiss of the espresso machine and the slap of the magazine pages the waitress was turning, but it was all far away, lost behind the voice of this strange character, telling his strange story. 'Anyway, I hurried inside as you can imagine but – thank the Lord – my wife and all my children were fine, in high health and spirits, and over the next few days I began to think that perhaps it was the undertaker who had been drunk, and not me!' He sat back and laughed, and the sound chilled me. 'But then, and you see, sir, this is the part that has really disturbed me, then a few nights later I was feeling tired and didn't want to bother with the Red Lion, and so sat at home in the parlour with a bottle of Mild. It was cold, unseasonably, I thought, and as the wife was busy upstairs I lit the gas fire and settled into my armchair, and, well, after a few minutes I fell quite asleep. And even though I was asleep I thought the fire must have gone out as the cold was seeping into my bones, and pressing down on me, and in the end it woke me up – but I found I wasn't sitting in my chair, but lying down.' His face puckered at the memory. 'I struggled to sit up and I saw that I wasn't even at home, but I was in the street, sitting up in a coffin.' His eyes met mine and the fear was bright in them. 'A coffin! And all around me were these undertakers, carrying the coffin along, and they seemed very tall and distant, their faces all – calm, like. Well, I started shouting, make no mistake! *"Stop! Stop!"* and for a long while it didn't seem they would stop but in the end the tallest one, who I saw was the man I'd spoken to from the carriage, he looked down at me and said: *"We've come a little early, sir, just a little early,"* and with that I found myself sitting on the road in the middle of our street in all the wet, with no-one about at all.' I stared at him, and he nodded, and began to collect up gloves and a hat from beside his table as if somehow he'd done what he'd meant to do and could now leave.

'But what happened? Who were they?' I said, grabbing at his sleeve, which released another powerful waft of mothballs and that under scent of – decay, I realised with a jolt. The little man was standing now, and he didn't seem little anymore.

'Well, sir, of course after that I didn't want to fall asleep – oh ho, no! I didn't want to fall asleep at all! Every time my eyes closed, no matter whether I was sitting up or lying in my bed, each and every time I felt that coldness start to clutch at me, close in on me, and I would jump up and walk about and try to wake up.' He stopped, and slowly placed onto his head a tall, black hat. A long knot of black crepe hung down from the brim, and draped itself down the back of his coat. He stooped down, and I felt the weight of his hand pressing into my shoulder as he whispered to me: 'But you can't stay awake for ever, can you, sir?'

My eye flicked to the misty window, and I saw my own reflection, wide-eyed and ghostly, but only mine. In my ear I heard his voice chuckling: 'I'll see you again, sir, I've just come a little early, just a little early'.

And then I was alone, and the warmth of the café faded away, curdling into a terrible, aching cold…

SIGN HERE

'Sign here, please.' Mr Carbody held out the pen, and then gestured with it impatiently when Steve didn't take it at once. Slowly, the young man unfurled his fingers from the tight fist they had formed, and accepted the heavy gold ballpoint. His hand moved across the white page, and lined up with the row that Mr Carbody – soon to be his new boss, he realised with a start – was pointing towards. 'Just here,' he said.

Steve's mind jumped backwards to the conversation he'd had with Pete that morning. Could it only be this morning? The memory seemed to be coming from miles away, beamed across the universe from a distant star. He and Pete had been in the coffee shop down the road from their flat, gloomily searching for jobs on their phones, and having a perverse sort of competition to see who could find the job most unsuited to their own limited skills.

'Hey, look at this one,' Pete had said, holding old his battered iPhone with the cracked screen. Steve peered past the fractures.

'Customer-service role with global company, based in Holborn,' he read. 'What's wrong with that?'

Pete snorted and snatched the mobile back to scroll to the offending text. 'Must speak fluent English and at least one other European language to degree standard'. Huh! We barely speak English to degree standard!'

They both sighed. Steve let his hand drop over the side of his squashy armchair. Perhaps his mum had been right when she'd suggested he leave London and come back to Sheffield. His eye fell onto the half-drunk cappuccino sitting on the low table, and the sight of the sticky brown tide encircling the heavy white cup made him feel slightly sick. He'd been nursing the drink for an hour, and already the baristas were casting unfriendly glances his way. His gaze flitted up to regard his friend. He was chatting and flirting with a young waitress, who was pretending to coolly ignore him whilst actually flirting back. Steve frowned. It was alright for Pete. He had money of his own, so this enforced limbo between uni and career was just a kind of scabby holiday: something to be laughed about later, in that strange, middle-class reverse boasting sort of way.

His phone, held slack in his hand, beeped. Automatically Steve turned his wrist and read the message. It was an email from one of the myriad jobs' sites he'd signed up to. Admittedly, he didn't recognise the website's name – signonthedottedline.biz – but he'd set up alerts on so many of these things that wasn't really surprising he didn't remember this one.

> STOP PRESS! London-based international company are looking for an accounts executive to join their busy office. Competitive salary and benefits. One vacancy available. Interested?
> Apply Now!

A large, red button sat at the bottom of the email, just inviting him to push it. Again, Steve's eyes cut to his friend, who was now exchanging contact information with the pretty waitress. His thumb hovered over the button, just for a second, and as Pete's well-bred laugh brayed out loudly he set his mouth in a hard line and pushed.

Immediately the message vanished from the screen, and an instant later the phone buzzed as a text message came in:

Hi Steve, thanks for your application. Please come for an informal interview at 12.30 TODAY. 19 Marshall Street W1F.

Steve sat up in his chair. The clock above the baristas' counter was already showing 11.45 – he'd have to rush to get there on time. He couldn't miss this. It was his big chance. He stood up and started picking up his bag and struggling into his coat.

'What's happening?' asked Pete, half rising to his feet. 'Where are we going?'

'We're not going anywhere,' said Steve, finding his best friend suddenly very irritating.

Why didn't this loser just stop hanging around him? 'I am going to an appointment.'

Pete's shrewd eyes narrowed. 'You've got a job interview, haven't you?' He smiled and frowned. 'You jammy beggar. Why didn't you tell me? We could have both applied!'

Steve shrugged. 'There was only one job, and I need it more than you.' Then he smiled too, and Pete recoiled slightly from its nastiness. 'You snooze, you lose. See you around.' And then he was off, striding past the idiots drinking their over-priced froth, and bashing through the glass doors and onto the pavement. He should have done this ages ago, he thought as he ran down into the tube station, he should have ditched that posh moron and just struck out on his own. He smiled to himself as he stood, swaying, in the train, and didn't notice how his strange expression was creating a little vacuum of space around him where the other passengers had instinctively edged away.

He was marching down Marshall Street at 12.25, and his phone beeped. It was another text.

> Hi Steve, thanks for being so prompt. Please push the door to number 19 and come up to the second floor. Ignore the hard hat sign. See you shortly.

He stopped dead, to the annoyance of passers-by, and frowned at the phone. How did they know he was here? Were they tracking this phone? Or were they watching him? He looked up and stared apprehensively up and down the road, half expecting to see someone smile and wave, but there was no-one. Well, no matter, he needed to hurry now. He walked the last few paces, past a sign saying something about a plague pit being found under the street, and located the door to the building tucked behind a skip and behind some scaffolding. As the message had warned him, a large red and white notice shouted that this was a restricted area and hard hats must be worn on site. Steve hesitated, until a gust of wind blew an appaling stench into his face from the pile of bloated and glistening white garbage bags which filled the skip like huge cancerous tumours, and he almost dived through the doorway to get away.

Inside the hallway, the door swung behind him and locked with a click.

Ahead, a battered flight of stairs led upward into gloom. Steve paused. The whole building looked in terrible repair, with broken floorboards and tufts of exposed wiring pulled out from the walls. Perhaps he shouldn't go up. Perhaps this was all a hoax. Perhaps... His phoned beeped again.

Hi Steve. We are waiting for you on the second floor. Please hurry.

Steve found his feet hammering the wooden stairs as if they'd decided to respond to the message all by themselves. His mind felt strange, floating and remote, slightly detached from his body. Semi-detached, he thought, and had to fight down a gale of hysterical laughter that swept through him. What the hell was he doing, anyway? He'd been really rude to Pete and...

...the stairs turned and suddenly he was pushing through an old fire door and into a wide space, lit by the windows facing the street. The sounds of London floated in, but somehow washed out and faint. He stepped hesitantly forward, seeing no-one, and certainly not seeing the busy office promised in the job ad. Steve walked towards the windows, where sheets of translucent white plastic blocked the view and which crackled with every suck and gust of cold air. Beep, went his phone.

> Hi Steve. Please make your way to the back corner, where Mr Carbody is waiting for you in room 66b.

He turned and made his cautious way back across the empty floor to where, now he could see, a set of boxy offices had been installed. Signs on the doors told him that he was passing rooms 12, 13 and 15, and he jumped to see flickers of movement behind their frosted glass – he'd thought he was alone here in this silent, abandoned place. Inexplicably, the next office was numbered 66b, but where numbers 15 to 65 were, or indeed, 66a, he had no idea. A cold feeling was curdling in his stomach; he realised that if he ever told his mum about this appointment she'd shriek that he didn't know anything about this company, or this Mr

Carbody. He could be a mass murderer for all Steve knew. Then the door to office 66b was flung open, and a tall handsome man was standing there, smiling at him.

'Ah! Steve! Thanks so much for coming!' Steve found himself being ushered into the little room, and the door shutting behind him. 'Do sit down. Can I get you anything? Coffee? Water? No? Well, sing out if you change your mind.' The interviewer, Mr Carbody, he assumed, was all smiles and courtesy and it made Steve feel very embarrassed to have been caught in the act of wondering whether this debonair manager was in fact a serial killer. Mr Carbody winked, as if he'd read Steve's mind, and the young man jumped. 'All a bit unusual, this, isn't it?' He leaned forward onto the desk, confidentially. 'To be honest, our HR department blundered hugely and so had to send out the interview appointments this morning at the last minute.' He sighed and rolled his eyes theatrically, and Steve found himself relaxing and joining in the laughter. It was just an HR fuck up! So much for his psychopath theory.

Mr Carbody grinned, revealing a rather alarming set of large, white teeth, and then sat back in his chair. He regarded Steve thoughtfully, appraisingly, almost, and then said: 'So, what's the job? Well, I'll tell you, this type of position doesn't come up very often, Steve. This company, well, it's a rare beast. It can really look at a person and see their potential. We've got all your qualifications and references and so forth,' he waved an airy hand at the surface of the desk, which Steve now noticed was covered by papers that he was surprised to recognise as his own CV and some of the other job applications he'd filled in his week, 'but what matters to us is what's in here.' Mr Carbody laid a hand over his own heart. This must be an American company, thought Steve. 'Anybody can take exams and get degrees and what not, but here we see who you are, and what you're capable of, and we develop that.'

Steve felt a flush of hope run, warm, through his body. He'd always felt that if only he could have a chance to show what he could really do, if only people saw who he really was, then nothing would hold him back. Could this, finally, be the break he'd wanted for so long?

'That's, er, really interesting,' he said, trying to sound cool and not boyishly enthusiastic, 'but what is the role actually doing…'

'Good question! Excellent question!' Mr Carbody grinned and Steve wondered if he was going to reach across the desk to shake his hand. 'Well, that depends on the results of various psychometric and other tests that we run immediately on commencement of employment. And do you know, Steve, that not one candidate in a hundred would ask that question first? Not one!' He smiled, and Steve was reminded of the smiling wolf on the way to Grandma's house, but Mr Carbody was continuing with gusto. 'No indeed! Most people would ask what's in it for them? Remuneration, benefits, vacation time, company car, and so on.' Company car! Steve almost didn't dare to breathe. He carried on holding his breath as Mr Carbody named an extraordinary sum as the starting salary, and then dazzled Steve with a description of the holidays and expenses and use of luxury apartments that would be available to him, all delivered in a matter-of-fact tone as if these were standard perks that any entry-level graduate job would command. Steve, after six long months adrift in the jobs' market, knew otherwise. He could suddenly see himself, besuited and polished, stepping out of some outrageously expensive vehicle, and dropping in on Pete as he languished in his middle-class escapism of unemployment. Oh, how he'd love that!

He came back to himself to find the small, dark eyes of Mr Carbody watching him acutely. For the second time, he had an uncomfortable feeling that the interviewer was listening to his every thought. As this idea flitted across his consciousness, he was disconcerted to see the tall man break into a grin and wink.

'Well, Steve, what do you say?' Mr Carbody's eyes were very dark, Steve thought, and very deep, and staring into them he felt that sensation he'd only felt before when standing at the top of a high building, and inexplicably his head seemed too heavy to keep upright and he felt it would be so easy to just topple over and plunge down... 'some forms to sign.' Steve blinked; he'd completely missed that last bit, and now Mr Carbody was holding out a pen and gesturing towards a sheet of densely-typed paper that had appeared on the now empty desk. The man stood up, and he seemed taller now, even taller and lankier than before, which of course wasn't possible. Steve wiped his face with his hand, it was so blazingly hot in here, and he felt suddenly quite sick. The tiny lines of type on the contract swam and blurred in his vision.

'Could I have that glass of water, please?' he asked.

'In just a second. Sign here, please.' Mr Carbody held out the pen, and then gestured with it impatiently when Steve didn't take it at once. Slowly, the young man unfurled his fingers from the tight fist they had formed, and accepted the heavy gold ballpoint. His hand moved across the white page, and lined up with the row that Mr Carbody – soon to be his new boss, he realised with a start – was pointing towards. 'Just here,' he said.

Steve signed, and a sound like a huge collective sigh filled the air. He blinked up at the enormously tall Mr Carbody, who had dropped his smile and now looked almost pityingly at him.

'Welcome to the firm,' he said.

Later that afternoon Steve's phone beeped. It was a 'breaking news' alert that he'd set up from the BBC website, stating dispassionately that the dismembered body of a young man had been found on a building site in central London. The phone, which had slid down the side of the stinking skip and now lay in a puddle of yellowish fluid at the bottom, flashed the red and white message twice, and then went dark.

DR PAIGNTON

It was half-way through Hilary term in the year 1877 when my father died. I remember standing in the porters' lodge, reading the letter from my mother, and realising that my whole world had changed. We weren't a wealthy family, and with his death my father's small annuity had ceased. Felix, my older brother, was in the Indian Civil Service and it would be some months before he could return home to take charge; in the meantime, there was no option but that I come down from Oxford and take some employment that would keep my mother and younger brothers and sisters housed and fed. Selfishly, my first thoughts were bitter and angry that this responsibility should have fallen on me. The certainty of the Oxford term and the academic year were ripped away, and the bells ringing for Evensong that dark and blustery Sunday were no longer pealing for me.

With leaden steps I crossed First Quad and sought out my tutor, Dr Randall, before he could dash across to Chapel. Fortunately, he was running late as usual and was still in his rooms, and I blurted out my news without delay. I picture him now, standing tall and stork-like, with his arms half-in and half-out of his gown, listening to me explain how I had to leave and didn't know when, or indeed if, I would ever return to complete my studies.

'Please accept my condolences, Wimbourne,' he said, adjusting the black bombazine across his shoulders and gesturing me to take a seat in the armchair across from his own. I sat, feeling wretched that I was not more saddened by losing my father, but simultaneously recognising that I was already one apart, and would never have a tutorial in this room again. 'I sympathise also with the necessity for you to assume the mantle of provider for your family,' he went on. 'It is a burden that I share – as you know, I have a sister whom I support – and it is especially hard to grapple with that burden when one is so young.'

I explained that my brother would be returning to England as soon as it could be arranged, and would, no doubt, take up a position that would place him at the head of the family.

'Ah!' Dr Randall smiled at this. 'You find yourself in the role of temporary protector, only?' At my nod he clapped his hands cheerily. 'Well, then don't look so cast down, my boy! You may be back for the start of the Michaelmas term, and, with some small adjustments, you can resume your degree and pick up your scholarship once again.'

His cheerfulness began to penetrate the gloom with which I had wrapped myself. 'Do you really think so, sir?' I asked, but then another worry pierced me. 'But I still need to earn some kind of living till my brother is home, and frankly I have no more idea of how to do that than fly.' Vague ideas of newspaper advertisements calling for companions and secretaries flitted into my mind, in truth, more from the pages of popular fiction than from any personal knowledge.

'And there we must thank the Almighty for providing me with exactly what you need!' cried my tutor happily, springing energetically out of his chair and rummaging on his desk in a great storm of papers. 'I received this letter a week ago and have been considering my reply, and here you come like an answer to a prayer!'

He thrust a couple of closely-written pages into my hand. It took a moment to adjust my eyes to cope with the dense and spidery writing, but I turned to the fire for more light and began to read.

Dear Rudolph

I trust that this letter finds you in good health, and fine spirits. How is your Magnum Opus progressing? I own that, while I do not regret leaving my Chair, I do sometimes miss the communal feeling of College life; and I must envy your unfettered access to the treasures of the College and University libraries.

I am pleased to inform you that My Own Work continues apace, and with much success. I feel that I am now only a hand span away from breaking through the remaining occlusions that separate me from Greater Understanding. My efforts have been difficult, exhausting, and, at times, dispiriting, but all that is as nothing now the pinnacle of my endeavours is within sight. I know that you, my friend, were uneasy about my withdrawal from the world to this remote place, the better to continue my work undisturbed; I am glad to report that its privations and my wider sacrifices have not been made in vain.

It is to that end that I write to you. My strength is not what it once was, and I am experiencing some difficulties with my eyesight that have arisen, I have no doubt, from long hours of reading and study. I am therefore writing to enquire whether you know of any recent graduate who might come to Thursby and act as assistant, amanuensis, and secretary for a period of six months or until my work is concluded, whichever is sooner. I am in the position to be able to pay a monthly salary of ----, which I believe is slightly higher than usual, but which reflects the additional discomfiture that is attendant on living in this out-of-the-world spot. You know my field of study, and I am prepared to take any recommendation made by you as to a suitable young man as the judgement of Solomon himself.

The matter is pressing and so I await your reply at your earliest convenience. I remain, your friend and obedient servant,

Theodore Milgram Paignton

I put down the letter and stared in amazement at Dr Randall. 'Would you recommend me for this position, sir?' I cried.

'Of course, of course, you have one of the best minds of your year,' he said, 'when you choose to use it. Dr Paignton was a Fellow here for two decades, and retired last year to his family home in Yorkshire, the better to concentrate on completing his research. You are everything he could look for in an assistant.'

How I look back in bitterness at that moment! I can feel my own excitement and relief at the transformation of what had felt like a sentence of banishment into something approaching an adventure, with the reassuring spires of Oxford welcoming me back again at the end of it. I can see, in my mind's pitiless eye, the relief on the face of Dr Randall at being able to make a recommendation to his colleague, then then happily forget the matter and return to the embrace of his own work. What a stroke of good fortune it all seemed. I wish to God that I had not, in my laziness and enthusiasm, snatched at this first offer – but I never thought to question what appeared to be a golden opportunity.

In a few words, letters and telegrams were despatched with an urgency pleasing to my youth: to Dr Paignton in Yorkshire, to my mother, and even to Felix in Bangalore. By the following Friday I had packed up my room and left my trunk, corded and secured, with the porters against my return, and I was sitting in a third class compartment on the first of a series of trains that would take me to the remote village of Thursby in the Dales. I carried only a small bag, a dense volume on Chemistry given to me as a parting gift by Dr Randall, and such small funds as I had been able to muster once my battels and the other trifling debts of a student's life had been paid. I stared out of the sooty window at the backs of the mean houses in Birmingham and Doncaster and Sheffield, and then at the tiny, crouching villages set amongst the wild expanses of brownish moorland, and wondered at this incredible interruption to my peaceful world of golden Colleges and soft, green Oxfordshire countryside. Galahad, or any of Tennyson's other knights, setting out on their quests, could not have been more excited.

By the time I had climbed out of the final train, stiff and cold, and onto the little platform at Thursby Heath, I had long since come to realise the difference between poetry and reality. I had been travelling for the best part of two days, including an overnight stay amongst shabby commercial travellers in a guest house in

York, and I felt dirty and dishevelled. My stock of coin had run alarmingly low, and so I'd had to forego any refreshments at the last major interchange and was, as a result, also very hungry. Put all together, I did not feel that I would be making any great or favourable impression on Dr Paignton, and I had begun to worry that he would send me straight home. I see now that this was mere anxiety, but at the time it seemed to be a very real prospect and I had to counsel myself to ignore it as I limped down to the only vehicle waiting by the station entrance, a dilapidated trap.

'Good evening,' I said politely to the giant of a man lounging at the horse's head. 'My name is Lawrence Wimbourne, and I am Dr Paignton's new secretary.' The man gave no reply to this save a profound scowl. I pressed on. 'I was given to understand that transport would be provided to take me to Thursby Grange?' Again, silence. At last my temper snapped. 'Are you Dr Paignton's man, Barrett, or are you not?'

The giant moved, straightening himself up in the deep gloom of approaching dusk. I saw he was even larger than I had first appreciated. 'Aye,' uttered this colossus, 'there's no need for rudeness, young master, you just had to ask me.'

This, as it turned out, was nearly the most words uttered together that I ever heard from the man. We passed the journey to my new place of employment in silence, and as the casual talk about the doctor that I had imagined would take place on this final leg of my travels was absent, I instead listened to the creak of the carriage, and the plodding of the horse, and to the eerie whistling of the wind as it swept over the dead brown heather and – it seemed - straight down the neck of my Ulster. Night had fallen, such a profound blackness that I, a town dweller all my life, had never known; the carriage lamps were feeble amongst such an eternity of darkness and I could not understand how the coachman or indeed the horse could see their way across the dismal moor. What felt like hours passed, and I began to wonder if I were in fact dead and this bubble of light with the trap and the horse were transporting me to the afterlife, with Barrett a very fitting figure of Charon.

I think I must have fallen asleep in the end, for I was very fatigued from my journey, and the next thing I knew the tall man was rudely shaking my shoulder and pointing me towards another, brighter lamp held aloft by a short, elderly woman. I stumbled from the trap, hardly knowing whether I was coming or going, and the figure with the light resolved before my eyes into a soberly dressed housekeeper with an old-fashioned white cap upon her head. She was eyeing me warily, and I tried my best to straighten up and look respectable.

'Mr Wimbourne?' she asked, uncertainty in every syllable. I smiled, which did not appear to reassure her.

'Yes, and you are?'

'Mrs Marsden, I keep house for Dr Paignton.' The expression on her face was strange, almost like fear. I hoped I did not look as disreputable as all that. The woman did not move, and I glanced to either side.

'Is Dr Paignton here?' I asked.

'He's... in bed, sir,' she said, again with a flash of something under her conventional words, 'and sends his compliments. He will see you on the morrow.'

'Indeed,' I was childishly peeved that the man hadn't bothered to wait up for me. 'Well, Mrs Marsden, may I come in? I am tired and cold, and have been travelling for many hours.'

At this the housekeeper gave herself a shake and, apologising, led the way under a low stone arch and into the kitchen. Compared to the vacuum of the moor, the bright candles and the scrubbed table seemed a very temple of civilisation.

'I hope you do not mind eating in the kitchen, sir,' she went on, as a young and silly-looking maid took my bag and helped me off with my overcoat, 'but the master has already dined.' I sat down and she set a plate with a thick wedge of pie and a heap of hot buttered potatoes in front of me and then handed me a tureen of vegetables.

'Not at all, Mrs Marsden,' I said, and set to making the most of her hospitality. 'For this banquet I would happily eat with the Devil himself.' There was a clatter as housekeeper dropped the lid onto the tureen, and it broke. Her face was pale and she tutted angrily at herself as she cleared the shattered pieces. I felt a wave of embarrassment that I had unthinkingly spoken coarsely, as if I were amongst my peers in College. 'I beg your pardon, I have offended you. Please accept my apologies; I am very weary and this has made me careless with my tongue.'

She nodded an acceptance of my words, but the rest of the meal passed in uneasy silence. As I ate, I could see the housekeeper twisting and twisting a cloth she held in her hands, and at the back of the kitchen the maid, Elsie, fluttered nervously. Of Barrett there was no sign – perhaps he took his meals with the horse. At last I'd swallowed the final mouthful and drained my glass of beer, and Mrs Marsden suggested that she show me to my room.

Now that I was fed, I found that my exhaustion had collapsed on me with full force; as we walked through the Grange, lit only by the candle the housekeeper carried, it seemed the walls and floor were curved, and the darkened doorways grinned awfully, blackness on blackness. The floor was flagged, the staircase blackened with age, the ceilings higher than the light reached – all in all my memory of that first view of the place that would be of singular importance in my life is corrupted and confused. I know we reached a plain room and the woman lit a candle standing beside a narrow bed and then left and closed the door behind her, and I know I opened my bag to retrieve my night clothes, but after that there is nothing.

The morning brought all the usual ceremony of settling oneself into a new place; suffice to say that, once bathed, shaved and in a change of clothes I felt a good deal more like myself. I had slept profoundly, and was still yawning as I ate my breakfast in the kitchen. Of Dr Paignton, again there was no sign. Mrs

Marsden was evasive when I enquired after my employer, and repeated that he was resting and I would see him later.

I waited. After becoming bored waiting in my own room I set out to explore the house, and found it to be every bit as Gothic as I had been led to believe by my glimpses of it the evening before. I chuckled at the stuffed boars' heads and the suits of armour, the heavy oil paintings of (what I assumed) were Dr Paignton's noble ancestors and the crossed swords above the fireplaces, and resolved to describe it all to Connie, my youngest sister, in my next letter. More pertinently to me was the library, gloriously stacked floor to ceiling with volumes on subjects as diverse as anatomy, chemistry and the occult. On another day I would have happily have pulled a book off the shelves and thrown myself into an armchair, but I was full of youthful energy after two days cooped up in a train and so abandoned my wait for the mysterious doctor and went outside.

What a strange place is Thursby Grange! It has become quite notorious now, but in those days it was untouched, as untouched as the day when the Blackfriars had chosen it for their Abbey. Why they had selected this particular spot was a mystery to me – it seemed no different to anything I could see for miles around. Brown, peaty moors stretched out from horizon to horizon, broken here and there by deeply cutting streams; overhead the sky was a huge bowl of hazy blue, and as I watched I could see blowing in the clouds denoting a change to more turbulent weather. I had looked up Dr Paignton's home in *Historic Homes of England* before I had left College and now, as I wandered around the solid, slightly squat house, I could see the signs of its having been altered from the monastic building it had overtaken and subsumed. The Grange rambled over three main wings, but all appeared to be abandoned, save the portion nearest the kitchen that I had already explored. Glass was broken in the windows, roofs were slateless and partially collapsed, and gloom and darkness seemed to radiate from within. I peered into one downstairs room and saw only dust and cobwebs and shadows, and I shivered.

In truth, the desolation was not the only thing that made me shiver: even on this sunny morning the air was profoundly cold. My face and fingers burned with it, and my lungs were on fire as if I'd breathed in liquid glass. There was something else too, a very strong feeling that this strange place, this depression on the surface of the moor, were somehow thin, that the world as I knew it had worn out in this spot like the elbow on an old coat. I looked up at the wispy sky and for a second was absolutely convinced that my late father was looking down at me from Heaven and crying out to me in terrible anguish -

'Morning, master!' the ironic salute of Barrett the coachman pulled me out of these peculiar and blasphemous thoughts. Somehow, without realising it, I had wandered along to the stable yard where the tall man was engaged in the usual equine rites. His grin, as he passed me with a stinking and steaming wheelbarrow, was insolent. I chose not to rise to this baiting, and instead went back inside.

The rest of the day I spent as industriously as I could in writing letters. Huddled in my Ulster in my chilly bedroom, I wrote to my mother, asking her to send me woollen underwear, as well as the old set of tweeds that Felix had left behind and a pair of his sturdiest walking boots; I could not very well explore my new environment without suitable clothing. I wrote to Connie, and made myself chuckle describing the Grange and its strange inhabitants. Finally I wrote to Dr Randall, thanking him again for this employment. Letters written, I read until the light began to fail, and then the need for some life and company in this cheerless place led me to the kitchen.

Nothing was said about me dining with Dr Paignton, and instead I was slightly annoyed to find that a plate was set for me between silly Elsie and looming Barrett, as if I were merely another servant and this my rightful place.

Youthful pride made me consider rejecting these accommodations, and demanding that the dining room be set just for me, but youthful insecurity had me sit meekly down and eat the hearty but unsophisticated Irish stew that was tonight's menu. Conversation, such as it was, faltered and we mainly ate in silence; more than once I looked up to find the small, gimletly eyes of Mrs Marsden fixed on me with glittering force. I didn't bother to enquire about my employer.

So ended my first full day at Thursby Grange. I got quickly into bed, and huddled under the covers, wondering whether this was all some elaborate hoax, or test, and Dr Paignton did not, in fact, exist. I thought these angry thoughts would keep me awake but I fell asleep almost at once.

It was as dark as the grave when I woke. A hand was shaking me, its grip frighteningly strong, and I floundered amongst the blankets as I tried to fight away from what I assumed must be a nightmare. Then a match was struck, terrible in the blackness, and when my eyes cleared a little I saw that a small, thin old man was standing next to the bed, holding a candle.

'Wake up! Wake up, Mr Wimbourne! I pray you, wake up at once!'

Sleep fell from me in an instant, and I sat up. 'Dr Paignton?' I stared at the figure, and as I watched the candle was lowered with an awful slowness away from his face. I drew back at the little, wizened mask that peered at me from the gloom, its teeth slightly bared.

'Yes, yes! Come now, bestir yourself, sir; I will await you outside.' And the man and the light withdrew and the door clicked shut. Swallowed again by the darkness I fumbled to light my own candle, and then threw my clothes on any how. The cold was startling, and I thought that I was awake, but even as I finished lacing my boots and then advanced on the closed bedroom door I half expected to find no-one waiting for me in the passage, and this whole flurry be revealed as the remnant of some compelling dream.

Yet here was the little man and his candle, standing and waiting impatiently for me with his wrinkled monkey's face.

'Really, sir! I trust this laziness is not the measure of you!' Dr Paignton did not wait for me to speak, but turned and hurried into the black void of the corridor, requiring me to almost run to keep pace.

'But sir, it is past midnight! I did not know that –'

'The enormities of what you do not know must be a sore trial to you, Mr Wimbourne,' came the tart reply, and the doctor threw open a door into a room that I recognised to be adjacent to the library. 'This is my study, pray sit down.'

In a daze, I did as I was told. When I had glanced into it this morning, I had judged the room to be in disuse, but now a tiny fire burned in the grate and the dust seemed cleaned away. My employer lit an oil lamp on the table and another on the further bookcase, and I saw that there was a second door in the corner. Dr Paignton caught my glance and stepped up to me where I sat at the scored and well-worn desk.

'That is the entrance to my private room. Under no circumstances, sir, are you to enter that room. Under no circumstances, do you hear me?' I nodded, dumbly, and tried to stop my eyeballs from swivelling to stare at the forbidden door. 'The very Grange may stand in flames, sir, and you will not enter that room even to save my life. Is that understood?'

'I understand, sir.' The words were drawn out of me even as I was wondering what I should reply. The small, bent figure, dressed in old fashioned clothes and hardly as tall as my shoulder, was somehow very terrible. A dark fear bloomed in my chest and for a moment I had a clear thought of my father's ghost crying out at me to run, run... and then the doctor stepped away with a satisfied nod.

'That is good. Now, if you please, let us commence the work for which you are being handsomely paid.' He took up a sheaf of notes from the cabinet, and fixed a pair of pince-nez upon his nose. 'Paper and ink are in the drawer to your right hand. Take this dictation, Mr Wimbourne.'

The night seemed endless. For hours I scribbled notes that I hardly understood, then my employer had me fetch chemicals from a series of large glass jars stored in a cupboard, and mix them under his instruction. I had never handled such materials before, and Dr Paignton's views of my incompetency were scathing. The jars were heavy, my arms ached and shook, and the stink of the reactions left me retching, but on and on we went, until I thought I would faint or collapse. At last he drew back, his little yellow teeth bared with displeasure.

'It is no good! The final combination is not clear!' He paced up and down the tiny room, and I lowered my exhausted frame into the chair and held my head in my hands. The pacing and the grumbling rolled in my mind and I had almost fallen into the deep slumber of extreme fatigue when again his hateful, pinching hand gripped my shoulder. 'Wake up! Really, you are the laziest young man I have ever met! What Dr Randall meant by sending me such a dolt as you, I cannot say!' I struggled awake, and blinked in a sudden stripe of yellow sunlight that pierced the wooden shutters on the windows. The doctor's complaining shut off like a tap and he stepped slowly backwards towards the door to his own rooms.

'We have worked the whole night through, Dr Paignton,' I observed, trying not to yawn.

'Indeed, indeed. Well, hum, perhaps it is time to stop for now. But be awake at midnight, Mr Wimbourne, for I will need your wits sharp for tonight's researches!' He was almost invisible now in the gloomy corner. 'Get ye back to your bed.'

I needed no second invitation. In a moment I was stumbling out of the door and down the passage, past the servants' rooms where early morning stirrings could be heard, and then into my own bedchamber. Glorious golden light was streaming around the edges of the curtains, but I cared not, I fell across the bed and was asleep at once.

Later that morning I woke, my head splitting and my whole body afire with aches. I fumbled into a change of clothes, and then made my way to the kitchen. I was sorely ashamed by having slept so late, but my fatigue at the night's labours had given me no other choice. I sat at the table, not wishing to meet anyone's eye, and fell upon the plate of leftover stew that the housekeeper placed before me. As I ate, I could feel Elsie staring at me from the scullery doorway, and I was only glad that the dreadful Barrett wasn't also there to witness my embarrassment. It was only after I had finished eating that I noticed my hands were covered in tiny spots of black ink, and tiny dots of white where the acid from the chemicals had burned me. I shoved my fists under the table.

'Are you – are you alright, Mr Wimbourne?' I had not noticed Mrs Marsden approach, and I jumped and split some coffee into my saucer.

'Er, yes, thank you. I really must apologise for rising so late, it is not my usual habit, I do assure you –'

She cut off my protests with a gesture. I looked up at her strangely flat and expressionless face but thought I detected a gleam of sympathy in her eye.

'Do not trouble yourself, sir; Dr Paignton keeps strange hours and it was expected that you would be obliged to keep them with him.' She hovered, as if wanting to say more, but then stepped away and turned her back on me. 'Perhaps a walk this afternoon, Mr Wimbourne? It may – clear your head.'

I nodded, even though she was industriously cleaning the big stove in the corner and not looking at me. Then I gathered my Ulster and went outside into the cold. It had been raining, but for the present moment the skies had lightened a little and the wind was merely blustery. I wasn't dressed for hill walking – it would be a day or two before my brother's hand-me-downs could be expected to arrive in the post – but despite this my legs walked me out over the dead, brown moor and up to a slight promontory that I could see some distance from the Grange. Peaty water seeped into my shoes, and my trouser cuffs were soon soaked through, but the feeling of escape was blissful. I reached my goal, and scrambled up through the heather to stand on top. From here, a great nothingness was revealed, a whole panorama of bleakness. The wind, never still, whipped around me, making me so cold that I ceased noticing its bite. Most wonderful of all, for the first time since I'd climbed out of that train, I felt free. All at once I decided that I would immediately write to my mother and explain that the situation here was insupportable; that my employer was a man of dark habits and foul temper; and that I was leaving at once to return to Oxford. Let Felix make whatever arrangements he may to secure the family future, I had done enough.

Eventually the bitter weather quenched the fires of this youthful bravado, and I returned to the house. Mrs Marsden met me at the door, and handed me a letter that must have been delivered while I was on my walk. I recognised my mother's hand immediately, and tore it open. I won't repeat her words here, but sufficit to say that she humbly thanked me for sacrificing my academic career to provide for her and my siblings. She apologised for the difficulties this must be causing me, but blessed my employer for sending my quarter's wages in advance. I was shocked at the financial desperation hinted at by this overwhelming gratitude; in my Oxford bubble I had known nothing, had wanted to know nothing, of the grinding worry that she must have been experiencing. Guilt flamed in my chest, and then my heart sank with the realisation that I had to remain in Dr Paignton's service. It felt like a key turning in a lock.

The evening was terrible, a long desert of waiting. I could barely choke down Mrs Marsden's excellent dinner, and even the leering face of Barrett made no impression on me as I watched the hands on the kitchen clock crawl inexorably round. At last it reached eleven, and the servants began to make their preparations for bed. Without a word, the housekeeper had Elsie prepare a large jug of coffee for me, and then they all left the room. I sat alone, in the light of a single candle, and waited.

It was very quiet. I had seen no sign of my employer during the day, and yet I had no doubt that he was here, perhaps already stirring for his night's labour. I had brought a book from the library, but couldn't concentrate to read. Instead, I sat and counted the black and white spots on my hands, but I kept losing my place and having to start again. So engrossed did I become in this mindless occupation that I jumped nearly out of my chair when a knarled set of fingers clamped onto my shoulder.

'Here you are! Idling, sir, I catch you idling!' The crooked, monkey-like form of Dr Paignton stood before me and I experienced a physical revulsion so strong that I cringed away from him. He did not appear to notice, and instead chided and drove me from my chair and out into the dark corridors of the house. Luckily I'd had the presence of mind to snatch up the candle, for the doctor himself did not carry one, navigating the impenetrable blackness of the Grange by some other instinct, it seemed. We entered his study, and I bit down on my dismay as the door shut behind me.

When I attempt to describe my night's work in that place my words falter, and refuse to obey me. I cannot tell you why the notes and the measurements and the chemicals and the books of obscure writings filled me with such terrible dread; I cannot explain to you the appalling nature of the doctor's theories and his speculations about matters that any good Christian should leave well alone. Let me just say that each hour in his company felt like a year of my old life, and the very marrow of my bones revolted at his sneering face, his barbed and sarcastic tongue, and those long-fingered hands that slapped and grasped and prodded me to punctuate his displeasure. As on the previous night, I frantically scribbled notes to his dictation, read baffling excerpts from heavy volumes whose meaning was entirely obscure to me, and poured disgusting compounds from huge jars and demijohns into smaller and smaller vessels for him to peruse. My eyes burned from weariness and from the fumes, but he was never affected, and it was only the approach of daylight that prompted him to cease his demands and release me to my rest.

And thus was the pattern of my days firmly set. I would wake in the late morning, and stumble into the kitchen for a hot meal, served to me by a silent and brooding Mrs Marsden or by a giggling Elsie. Then, slightly revived by the food and by quantities of coffee, I would put on my brother's hand-me-down tweeds, sent to me by my grateful mother, and range over the desolate moor for hours. I ignored the gales and the rain that cut through my coat like knives, I ignored the biting cold, and the plentiful falls of snow that blew down from an endless white sky even late into May. I was driven, desperate to get out of the Grange and away from what I felt to be my captivity in its foul darkness. The icy wind scoured my mind and gave me, for those few hours of respite, a chance to be myself, to think for myself, and not be cowed by the terrible presence of Dr Paignton. Yet, while I scrambled over the marshy heather, I knew that I was merely a dog running on a long leash;

come six o'clock I must needs be back in my kennel.

In this way the days became weeks, and the weeks months, and Spring then Summer began to be felt even in this place where winter seemed always to reign. I tried to marshal the flickers of hope that these changes of seasons afforded; time was passing, and soon I would be back in the safety of my rooms in Oxford, and I could try to forget this period of my life in the way one tries to throw off the lingering taste of a terrible dream. Dr Paignton also appeared to change, becoming even wirier and thinner, and – judging by the declining strength of his pinching fingers – weaker too. Uncharitably I hoped he would fall desperately ill and be forced to remain in his bed, shut up in his private room beyond the study.

I had, under his dictation, written several letters of late to suppliers of chemicals and other equipment that he professed he needed for his work. Packages from Manchester and Edinburgh arrived almost daily, and unwrapping and installing these items made a welcome change for me during my nocturnal labours. I had expected that, as time went on, I would myself become knowledgeable about the doctor's research, but I confess that I had no more understanding of his obscure studies in August than I had had in March. Now, however, I knew that my time in his employ was running out, and so I dare say I had grown slightly careless when, on setting a delicate glass tap into the neck of a flask, I over tightened it and it cracked.

Dr Paignton was at my side in a second, faster than I could credit. 'Clumsy, careless boy! You imbecile! How dare you break my precious equipment in this fashion!'

'It was an accident –' I began to say, but he cut me off with a vicious grip on my arm. For all my youth and height his fingers bit into my flesh and the agony of it almost brought me to my knees. Dimly I wondered at this incredible strength, it was as unnatural as the rest of this macabre place. Then suddenly he released me, and sagged back into the chair like a collapsing balloon. Tentatively I stepped towards him but he held up an imperious hand to keep me at bay.

'Get to your rooms,' he whispered in a dreadful voice, 'at once! Leave me at once!'

Still hesitating, I stepped to the door, but he didn't call me back and I left him, and almost ran back to my bedroom. As I turned the key in the lock I was grasped by an atavistic horror at the whole scene, and I turned and pulled the heavy tallboy across the door. Only when it was in place did I feel myself relax. It was but three o'clock, I remember marking the time, and I was wide awake, for I was now as trained for night working as any watchman or janitor. Sleep was out of the question, so I huddled in my coat and began a long and desperate letter to my old tutor, Dr Randall, begging him to tell me that my place in College was safe and that I could return in October to resume my studies.

The candle had burned low and, despite my anxieties I must have dozed a little, when the hollow bump of the bedroom door against the set of drawers woke me in an instant. From where I sat, I could not see who – or indeed, what – stood outside.

'Who's there?' I cried, but there came no answer. Silence, heavy and threatening, filled my ears with a roaring and my heart drummed in my chest. 'Who's there?' I called again, and my strained hearing detected the sound of stealthy feet moving outside the door. I sprang up, the chair crashing to the ground behind me, and slammed the door shut with all my strength. I fumbled at the lock, turning the key again, and to my horror then saw it slowly unturn, as if controlled by the person on the other side. A force pushed at me, and I strained to push back, knowing in a panic that I wasn't strong enough, would never be strong enough, and then I heard a woman's voice from further down the passage calling out.

'What's happening?'

The door went slack against my hands and I thudded against it. For a long moment I stood there, trembling, but there was no further sound or movement, and at last I stumbled backward in a kind of faint and knew no more until morning.

I woke at my usual hour and threw open the curtains to a day of brilliant light. It had that crystal quality of the earliest Autumn, and I was suddenly convinced that I would be free of this place very soon. Felix, my brother, had wired me to say that he had, at long last, joined a ship leaving for England and he would be back in the next six weeks. Hope, beautiful, cruel hope, bloomed in my breast, and I went down to break my fast with a smile on my face.

I found the kitchen in an uproar. Mrs Marsden was sitting by the unlit stove, weeping into her apron; Barrett, scowling and surly as ever, was standing in the doorway and twisting his cap in his enormous hands; and most remarkable of all in this place that never changed, a young police constable was at the scrubbed kitchen table, taking laborious notes in a little book. He looked up and saw me.

'And who is this gentleman?' he asked, crossly. 'Are you Dr Paignton?'

'Good God! No!' I cried immediately, then at his surprised look, went on: 'I am Lawrence Wimbourne, assistant to Dr Paignton.'

'Ah!' he said, as if this was the breakthrough for which he had been searching. 'Aha!'

'What is going on?' I asked him, and when he did not answer, I crossed to the housekeeper and put my hand tentatively on her shoulder. 'Mrs Marsden, pray, what is wrong?' She shook her head, her face still covered by the white cloth.

'It's the lass, Elsie,' spoke up Barrett. I stared at him and saw fear in his little pale eyes. 'She's dead. Found up at Thursby Cross this morning.'

'Dead?' I repeated stupidly. 'But – how?'

'She was murdered, Mr Wimbourne!' The constable smiled at me horribly. I could tell that under his professional bluster he was enjoying himself immensely, and it made me feel ill.

'Murdered!' I sank into a chair. It didn't seem real, but then, nothing had seemed real since I came to this hateful place. I thought of

Elsie's cheerful face and silly laugh, and closed my eyes.

'Aye! Strangled she were, strangled and horribly mutilated!' The policeman rounded on weeping woman and almost shouted. 'And where is Dr Paignton? I must see him!'

Mrs Marsden dropped her hands and revealed her face, red and swollen with crying. 'He's not here! He's not been here for a month or more!' she said, astonishing me into silence. I opened my mouth to protest – surely he was this at this very moment asleep in his private room! – but the housekeeper turned and fixed a stare of such power on me that I fell silent. I wish to God I had spoken up then, but I did not.

The young constable's investigative technique appeared limited to shouting the same questions at us over and over, but Barrett remained mute, and Mrs Marden and I had no idea of what had happened to that poor, silly, fellow inmate of this dreadful house. He left, glaring at us in turn, and after a few seconds the coachman bolted as well. I turned at once to the housekeeper but she burst from her chair and ran from the room, leaving me sole master of the cold kitchen. I wondered if there was something I should do, some action that a grown man would take, but I'll own that I felt very much a boy, cast adrift amongst things I did not understand. In the end, falling back on some lesson learned in childhood, I lit the stove and boiled a kettle for tea.

I took a cup along the passage to Mrs Marsden's room and tapped on the door.

'Yes!' came a frightened voice.

'It's just me, Lawrence,' I said, and placed the cup and saucer on an oak chest where a candle waited for night-time. 'I've brought you some tea.' Silence greeted this statement, so I retreated to the kitchen and poured myself a cup, huddled close to the warming range and listening to the shriek and wail of the wind flying across the moor. The day was dying, and for the first time in hours I remembered that soon my employer would be waking and driving me on to work. I was just investigating the larder to see if there was something that I could eat prior to my night's labours when Mrs

Marsden came into the room. She carried the tea cup, now empty, and placed it carefully beside the sink. We both stood in silence, remembering that it would normally be Elsie who washed the dishes. Then the housekeeper tied on a clean apron and gestured for me to sit down.

'I'll make you some dinner, Mr Wimbourne,' she said. Neither of us felt much like eating, but the human frame demands its due, and she joined me to share the dish of broken meats and fried eggs that she had hastily created.

'You must forgive me, sir,' she said suddenly, startling me. I looked at her in surprise. 'No doubt you're wondering why I didn't tell the constable that Dr Paignton was here. I –' her voice broke, but she composed herself with an effort and continued, 'I cannot explain now, but I will explain in the morning.'

I stared at her. I didn't ask her to speak now; everything had reduced to the level of a nightmare, where the most outlandish statements or actions are taken completely for granted. Instead I just nodded, thinking that the morning felt like a long way away.

At eleven, Mrs Marsden banked the stove and left me with my single candle. I was not remotely sleepy, it was so horrible to be woken abruptly by the grinning face of Dr Paignton that there was no risk I would fall asleep. I watched the kitchen clock round till nearly midnight then walked calmly down to wait outside his study door. My employer had been so feeble of late that he'd taken to just calling out to me to come in, and so I jumped out of my skin when, a few minutes later, the door was flung open with such violence that it slammed against the wall with a boom.

'Wimbourne!' Dr Paignton stood in the entrance, lit by the small fire in the room beyond. I couldn't believe how changed he was: he stood taller than I'd seen him, his whole posture one of strength and energy rather than the slumped and exhausted frame I'd grown used to seeing. His face was alight with some kind of triumph that made my heart twist in my chest, and on observing my involuntary reaction, he laughed. May God save you from ever hearing a laugh such as that. 'Come in! Come in, my boy!' he chuckled, 'we have much work to do tonight!'

I stepped into the room with more than my usual reluctance, if that were possible, and tried to busy myself at the desk without looking him. There was something so wrong about his sudden vitality, something so unnatural about his wide grin and unfettered enthusiasm, that it made me shudder to my very soul. Of course, nothing escaped his notice.

'You perceive the difference in me, do you not?' he laughed at me. I nodded, still looking away, and hurriedly moved packages of powdered chemicals from where they were stacked on the floor onto the table top for decanting into the large jars. Dr Paignton roared with glee at my discomfiture. 'You do! You do! Well, I am restored, sir, quite, quite restored! What you may call a youthful energy is pouring through me! Ha! Ha!'

'How can that be possible, sir?' I almost whispered the question. At once, his grin of pleasure twisted into such a terrible grimace of fury that I took an involuntary step back and bumped the table behind me. One of the paper parcels, containing some yellow, sulpherish material, toppled from the surface and exploded across the floor in a starburst of stinking powder. I froze, horrified at this disaster.

For an anguished moment Dr Paignton did nothing, and then he drew in a long gasp that ended in a hiss and then a howl of monstrous rage. On and on went the scream, on and on, louder and longer than anything I'd ever heard, and I realised that it was no natural cry but the shriek of a demon from Hell itself. He did not stop to take another breath, indeed I now saw that he very rarely appeared to take a breath, and like the package tumbling to its destruction my mind plunged from safety and shattered on the horror of this new reality. This creature who had tormented me for so long was no longer human!

I shudder to consider what might have happened next, but the door flew open behind me and to my shock, Mrs Marsden ran into the room. She looked from my white, staring face to the explosion of yellow powder on the floor, and from thence to her master's shrieking mask.

'Stop! Stop!' she cried, and I saw that she held a poker in her hand, snatched up as if ready to attack a burglar. Without pausing, she took a step and brought the steel rod down upon Dr Paignton's head with a crack. For a second, we all stood as frozen, and then, horribly, oh how horribly, the doctor smiled an awful smile and began again to laugh.

'Do you think you can stop me with such flea bites?' he screamed, even as we stared at the long dent of broken bone and blackish blood that marked his brow. 'Nothing can stop me! Nothing! I have drunk deep of life itself and now I can continue my researches until they are concluded, even if it takes another hundred years!' He snatched up the poker and bent it effortlessly into a knot, laughing his demon's laugh all the while.

'Why did you kill Elsie?' cried the housekeeper, weeping and wringing her hands, 'Why? Why?'

He grinned then, a slow, dreadful grin and his little monkey eyes looked at me. 'Why? Because I needed young blood to revive me, of course, and because Mr Wimbourne blocked his door.' My own blood ran cold at this and I staggered away, gasping. I was responsible for the poor girl's death! My reason left me for a second, and the sound of the doctor's terrible laughter and Mrs Marsden's weeping faded away, and then I breathed again and it all came rushing back – and with it came a cold rage of my own.

'Enough! Enough, you monster –' I saw I was leaning on the bookcase nearest the door to his private chamber, and I reached over and turned the handle. It was not locked, and I had a surge of burning triumph to see the panic cross the doctor's wizened features.

'No! Do not enter that room!' he shrieked, but I'd snatched up the oil lamp and turned and entered the chamber. Oh God! The sight still lives behind my eyes and in my dreams! I still smell the rot and the breath the dust and feel the sensation of the thousand cobwebs that choked the small space and cocooned the high back chair that stood in its centre. Under the shadowy veils of webs I saw the body of Dr Paignton, dead, dead, long dead, dried and desiccated and shrivelled, its eyes decayed and its wizened lips drawn back in a snarl.

Remotely, I heard the long scream of the housekeeper, but I did not pay it any mind. The doctor that I knew, the not-dead man, was clawing and scratching at my back to get me away but I lifted the lamp and plunged it into the heart of the corpse. It sprang at once into angry flames, the figure in the chair all but consumed, and I staggered back from its sudden heat while the joint screams of my companions met in my mind and everything turned white and I fainted.

The rest is quickly told. I came to myself, lying on a sacking bed in the cell of the local gaol. The constable had returned in the morning, accompanied by a dozen extra men, and they had found Elsie's bloodied clothing stuffed under my bed. Mrs Marsden, who could have told them that it was her employer who had killed the poor girl to suck in her life to rejuvenate himself, was run quite mad. Barrett, whom I am sure assisted his master in disposing of the maid's body and placing her clothes in my room, had vanished in the night, presumed lost on the moor. Only I was left, lying insensible on the study floor, with the blackened body of Dr Paignton beside me.

The police surgeon declared that I was in a deep form of shock, but would soon recover. The doctor, however, had clearly been dead for many months – there is no surprise to learn they suspect it of being at my hand. As he was dead all this time, the orders for chemicals and the letters to suppliers have been, they think, some scheme of personation on my part, although to what end they cannot say. I awoke in hope that my long imprisonment at Thursby Grange was over, but it seems that Fate has one more joke to play upon me.

In vain did I protest that I had had no notion that the doctor was dead, that he'd been dead in fact before I even reached the Grange.

In vain I called for them to speak with Mrs Marsden, who could confirm that she, too, had seen the spirit we'd both believed to be the living man. A lawyer, sent from York, had shaken his head and told me that there was no use persisting with such a tale, and had entered a plea of Not Guilty for me at the Assizes. I wept and cried, and called upon God as my witness, but no-one believed me, and with Mrs Marsden insane, and Barrett run off, there was no-one to confirm my innocence. Needless to say, the trial was swift; the judgement of the twelve scowling Yorkshiremen implacable. Yet worst of all by far was the look on the face of my brother, Felix, just returned to England, who sat as stone in the courtroom and left after the verdict without even a word to me.

And so this tale is at its end. I hang tomorrow. I despair of my immortal soul, and even while I pray for mercy from Almighty God, I fear that when the veil of life is torn from my eyes, the first face I will see on the other side will be that awful, wrinkled mask of Dr Paignton.

ABOUT THE AUTHOR

Alex Marks has lived in Oxford for almost twenty years. A voracious reader, Alex consumes everything from thrillers to ghost stories, and from fantasy and science fiction to counterfactual tales.
Alex has been compulsively writing since childhood.

This is Alex's first volume of short stories. Visit Amazon for the novel 'White Light' and, in Spring 2017, for 'Shift Ten', a science fiction ghost story set in a future Oxford.

@IamAlexMarks | iamalexmarks.tumblr.com

ALEX MARKS

Printed in Great Britain
by Amazon